Addicted

to

You

Nikki Rittenberry

Manufactured in the United States of America

ISBN: 978-0615611358

"You can close your eyes to the things you do not want to see, but you cannot close your heart to the things you do not want to feel."

—Johnny Depp

Addicted
to
You

Prologue

Kendall Porter closed the pharmacy doors early in anticipation of the evening ahead. The small town of Butler Island never swayed from tradition, and welcoming a new year was no different. The annual festivities included a massive bonfire on the beach, followed by an elaborate fireworks display at the stroke of midnight over the calm Gulf of Mexico. The celebration was a B.Y.O.B.A.T. event (bring your own beverage and tree). Many residents brought their Christmas trees to the beach to fuel the bonfire, saving the city the burden of purchasing firewood for the affair.

Making a brief pit stop at home, Kendall quickly removed her more conservative work attire and changed into a beige cotton blouse and a faded denim skirt. And after touching up her make-up, she grabbed what was left of the six-pack of Corona from the fridge and headed to the beach.

She prayed the crowd—and the beer—were enough to ease the void. Her best friend, Olivia, had skipped town just before Christmas to photograph a

ski lift collapse in New Hampshire and had returned
to her apartment in New Orleans after having spent
the last two and a half months here. Olivia was a
freelance photographer, accustomed to traveling on a
moment's notice whenever tragedy struck, although
Kendall knew Olivia's abrupt departure probably
had more to do with avoiding Grant Womack than a
good photo op. He'd fallen head-over-heels in love
with her best friend. And even though Kendall's
intuition told her that Olivia felt the same way, the
girl was too stubborn to outwardly admit it.

Finally arriving at the beach, Kendall popped
the cap of her Corona with the bottle opener attached to her keychain and willed her body to move
toward the congregation of people already gathered
by the shore. The party was in full swing, the gentle
breeze wafting the sounds of country music and
light-hearted conversation through the airy night.
Hundreds of islanders mingled around the epic
bonfire, although not for warmth. It was the last day
of the year—winter—and it was a balmy seventy-
three degrees. Typical Florida winter weather: cool
one day, muggy the next.

Weaving through the crowd, she caught up with
some of her girlfriends.

"Kendall!" Jenny shouted as she approached. "Will
you please explain to Vicki that she needs to invest
in a pair of thongs? The girl thinks it's perfectly ac-
ceptable to parade around in those tight shorts with
a pair of granny panties underneath."

"They're not granny panties"—Vicki interjected—
"they're *bikini cut.*"

"Huh-uh, let's let the town's fashionista have
the final say."

Jenny placed her hands on Vicki's shoulders

and spun her around so that her derriere was illuminated by the fire. "Whatcha think?"

Kendall inspected the very visible panty lines. "Vicki, honey... I think it's time we went lingerie shopping together."

"Is it really that bad?"

"I'm afraid so."

Vicki sighed and then reached into her beach bag for her sweatshirt. She quickly tied it around her waist and then took a pull from her beer. "Well, I reckon this'll have to do the trick until then—although I'm not sure how comfortable I'm gonna feel with a piece of string wedged between my ass cheeks. I'm probably gonna attract more attention pickin' at the darn thing!"

"You won't feel a thing. And trust me, Alex will be putty in your hands when he sees you in them!" Kendall reassured her.

"When I see her in what?" Alex asked as he approached from behind.

"It's a surprise."

Alex wrapped his arms around Vicki's waist and nuzzled his face in the crook of her neck. "Mmm, I *love* surprises..."

Kendall observed the two lovebirds as they whispered sweet nothings to one another—hugging and kissing—utterly oblivious about the fact they had an audience. And before long, Jenny's husband, Tommy, and Lana's husband, Jimmy, had joined the group as well.

For the first time in recent memory, Kendall felt oddly out of place.

The third wheel.

It suddenly became clear that in the circle of

friends she surrounded herself with, she was the only single gal left. Single. Alone.

Would the upcoming year bring more of the same?—long hours at the pharmacy and countless nights spent alone?

Excusing herself from the small crowd of snuggling couples surrounding her, Kendall shuffled back to her car. She reached into the passenger seat for her last beer, removed the cap, and then slowly journeyed back to the beach.

Confidence: something she'd always had in abundance was now lacking. She was beginning to wonder if she'd ever find a man that wasn't threatened by her brains and boldness...

Moving away from the celebration, Kendall drifted toward the shore, sloshing her bare feet in the cool saltwater. Could this evening get any worse? In fact, why was she still here? She had no one to share a New Year's kiss with; no one to cuddle up against during the fireworks display.

Stopping for a moment, she gazed at the moon's reflection in the Gulf, pondering her next move, and then raised the bottle to her lips.

"The crowd gettin' to you too?" Ty asked as he quietly approached from behind.

Startled, Kendall spilled the beer down her chest and gasped as the frigid, frothy liquid soaked through her cotton blouse.

"Shit—I'm sorry! I didn't mean to scare you!"

"It's alright", she assured him as she stared at her chest.

Ty gestured toward her blouse. "Your shirt's, uh, soaked."

Kendall met his gaze and smiled. "Guess I should take it off then, huh." She shoved her nearly empty beer bottle toward his chest. "Do you mind holding this?" Without giving him an opportunity to object, she reached toward the front of her shirt and began unbuttoning.

Holy shit!

He was torn: be a gentleman, allowing Kendall some privacy, or sit front row to a private strip show... His eyes glazed over, unable to stray from her delicate manicured fingers as they worked to unbutton her damp blouse.

Sensing his internal struggle, Kendall set out to reassure him. "Relax, Ty, I'm wearing a camisole underneath—"

"Right. Yeah. Of course, you are..."

Shrugging out of her blouse, she quickly wrapped it around her waist, reached for her Corona and swallowed the remainder (which wasn't much, considering she was wearing most of it).

"Looks like you're out of beer."

"Looks that way."

Ty tossed his head back and swallowed the rest of his, wiping his beer-moistened lips with the back of his hand. "Well, then, that makes two of us. Why don't we do somethin' about that?"

"I'm listening..."

Ty smiled. "I happen to know—for a fact—that Grant stocked his fridge full of beer before he left town yesterday."

Kendall crossed her arms and studied him for a few long beats. "So, what—you wanna break into his beach house and steal his beer?—is that your brilliant plan?"

After reaching into his pocket, Ty dangled a key in front of her face. "It's not breaking and entering if

I have a key. And besides, he owes me." He could almost see the wheels turning in that pretty little mind of hers. "C'mon, you're not gonna make me drink alone tonight, are you?"

Kendall raked her teeth against her bottom lip and then smiled. "Alright, lead the way."

The two walked the short distance to Grant's beach house in relative silence, snagged two beers from the fridge, and then retraced their steps back to the beach.

"Have you heard from Olivia yet?" she asked as their feet unhurriedly waded through the frigid saltwater.

"Talked to her yesterday. She called to let me know she made it back safely." He paused for a few moments, debating whether or not to share details of Olivia's birthday surprise. "Can you keep a secret?" he finally asked.

"Of course."

Why he asked, he didn't know; Kendall wasn't the gossiping type. "Grant left yesterday to head to New Orleans. He's gonna surprise her."

"Are you serious?" She questioned. "Wow... It takes a rather large set of cojones to go toe-to-toe with that girl!"

"You're telling me", he commented wryly. Ty went on, divulging the details of the birthday gift Grant had put together for her, outlining how the surprise would unfold. "What do you think?"

"About Olivia and Grant?—well, I think what they have is the real deal. I just pray she's not too stubborn to go for it."

"Yeah, me too..."

Kendall chuckled softly under her breath as they came to a halt, their feet still submerged in the ocean.

"What's so funny?" Ty insisted.

"Nothing, it's just... when we were kids, we used to talk about what our *dream guy* would look like. Now that I think about it, Grant looks an awful lot like the fantasy guy she described."

"Really?" Ty took a step toward her and shifted a strand of hair away from her eye. "And what about you?"

Kendall swallowed hard, praying her voice wouldn't tremble. "What about me?"

"What did *your* fantasy guy look like?"

Maybe it was the way the moonlight settled across his handsome face, or the way his intoxicating masculine scent mingled with the calm, salty breeze. Or maybe it was the beer—truthfully, it didn't matter. She'd had a secret crush on Ty for as long as she could remember, and right now she was going to cease the moment. "It's funny you should ask. Because he looks an awful lot like you."

Ty's mouth turned upward in a sexy grin as the countdown to the New Year began in the distance.

"*Ten, nine, eight...*"

His mouth drew closer to hers.

"*...three, two, one.*"

"Happy New Year, Kendall", he whispered. Ty inched forward until his mouth pressed against hers. Her lips were soft, sensual.

The epitome of perfection.

And then those pouty lips parted in an invitation—one he dutifully accepted.

How many nights had she dreamt of kissing this man as a teenager?—as an adult? It was everything she imagined it would be and more. His rhythm. His gentleness. The way he tangled his fingers in her hair.

She tasted like unadulterated sin, sexy woman, and the finest imported beer. A potent combination that sent a fiery ball of lust to his groin. He tangled his fingers in her hair: black silk. Her free hand dug into his shoulder as his mouth migrated to her jaw, and then her neck. Her skin was smooth, delicious, and her scent, orange blossoms, roused a hunger that'd been dormant for months.

And then his mouth came over her lips again. This kiss was hot, fierce—predator-like.

Kendall heard a soft, carnal whimper and suddenly realized it'd come from her. She felt the vibrations from the fireworks exploding over the Gulf, but she didn't need to watch.

Nosiree.

Sensual explosions of colorful light detonated behind her eyes. Never before had she been kissed like this. A powerful electric current zipped down her spine and settled low in her gut, heightening her senses. And then as quickly as the surge materialized, the electric current faltered.

Ty tore his mouth away from her lips.

Had he really just kissed Kendall Porter?—his little sister's best friend? The same girl that used to come over for sleepovers with Olivia as a kid?

Ah, shit. "Sorry, I shouldn't have done that—"

"I-it's okay—"

Ty ran his hand through his hair and then shook his head. "No. You're... I'm..." He took a few steps back and then shoved his hands in his pockets. "I should go."

And that's how the New Year began: a euphoric high, followed by a painful—and rather embarrassing—withdrawal.

Chapter 1

Kendall Porter sat across from her childhood best friend, Olivia, in a booth at the local diner, meticulously adding the perfect ratio of sugar and cream to her morning cup of joe.

"I have somethin' really important to tell you", Olivia announced.

Kendall paused for a moment before stirring her coffee. "You mean, you're finally going to apologize for skipping town in the middle of the night last month without a backward glance? I was worried sick about you!"

Olivia gently placed her mug on the table and then reached for Kendall's hand, giving it a reassuring squeeze. "I really am sorry for not sayin' goodbye. That's just how my job works, though. I'm sort of at Mother Nature's mercy. I never meant to cause you to worry like—"

Kendall gasped as she glanced at Olivia's hand. "Holy shit!—that looks an awful lot like an engagement ring on your finger, Liv."

Unable to hide her growing grin, Olivia smiled,

her happiness beaming brighter than the overhead
fluorescent bulbs. "Well, that's because it is. Grant
asked me to marry him. And... I said yes!"

Covering her mouth with her free hand, Kendall's
eyes widened. "I really hope you're being serious right
now", she warned, her voice muffled by her palm,
"because this would be an incredibly cruel joke!"

"Of course, I'm being serious! In fact that's one of
the reasons I invited you to breakfast this morning. I
was wondering if you'd be my maid of honor?"

"Only under one condition: You won't make me
wear a frou-frou, Pepto-Bismol-colored, gaudy-looking
bridesmaid dress!"

"You've got yourself a deal!" Olivia picked up her
mug and took a sip before steering the subject toward
the other reason for her breakfast invitation. "So... I
ran into Lana yesterday..."

"Oh yeah?"

"Uh-huh. She mentioned you had a rather
exciting New Year's kiss with a mystery man. Anyone I might know?"

Damn this small island and all the loudmouth's
that lived on it! She'd been far enough away from the
crowd. Didn't think anyone had seen them. But she
should've known better. The women in this town were
equipped with gossip radar—like it was embedded in
their DNA or something. "It really wasn't a big deal,
Liv. To be honest, I completely forgot about it."

Liar. She hadn't forgotten about that kiss. In
fact, she'd spent the last two weeks replaying every
blissful second of it in her mind.

"You're lying—it's written all over your face!"

"Is not."

"Is, too!" Olivia countered.

The waitress arrived with their breakfast and

placed their ticket face down on the tabletop. She removed a bottle of ketchup from one of the pockets on the front of her apron, handed it to Kendall, and then disappeared behind the swinging doors to the kitchen.

"Alright", she reluctantly conceded as she shook the glass jar of ketchup over her eggs and onion rings. Yes, *onion rings*; she was addicted to the darn things. "Maybe it *was* sort of a big deal to me… Doesn't really matter, though. He's—hmmm, what's the word?" she uttered as she stroked her chin. "Inconveniently unavailable."

Olivia took a bite of her toast and carefully studied her. "He's married", she stated flatly.

"Well, it's sort of… *complicated.*"

This time Olivia gasped. "You lil' slut", she teased. "I think I know who the mystery man is!"

Ty sat outside on the deck at Grant's beach house, staring at the man that would soon become a permanent member of his family. It was sort of funny when he thought about it, really. Just last month he'd been on the verge of jamming his fist down Grant's throat for dating his little sister behind his back. Before Olivia, Grant hadn't exactly had the best reputation with women. Ty had assumed that Olivia was just another meaningless lay—a warm body in Grant's bed.

How wrong he'd been.

Never had he seen his sister—or his best friend, for that matter—look happier.

Grant eyed Ty over the rim of his coffee mug. "I know what you're thinking. You want to throw a big shindig."

"Liv deserves nothing but the best."

Refusing a chair, Grant took a seat on the deck railing. "On that, we agree. She *is* marrying *me*, after all", he stated with a wry grin.

"Good to know your ego's still intact."

Laughing, Grant placed his coffee mug beside him on the railing. "Listen, she wants to keep this whole wedding thing simple. And honestly I couldn't agree more."

Ty tapped his fingers to a beat only he could hear on the patio table, allowing the request to sink in. "When?"

"We were thinking of doing it in early April."

"Holy shit, man—that's less than three months away! That doesn't give us much time to—"

"We don't need a lot of time", Grant interrupted. "We want the ceremony and the small reception to be held here on the beach. Aside from her dress, food and drinks, everything is pretty much settled."

Nodding his head, Ty conceded. He wasn't surprised that Olivia wanted an understated, simple wedding; she wasn't a flashy kind of girl. She was undemanding, easy-going. Carefree. And a big, elaborate wedding represented everything she wasn't. "Alright, nothing fancy."

"Good. I'm glad we cleared that up." Grant took a sip of coffee and then placed his mug next to him on the rail. He'd been back for a few days and couldn't help but notice that Ty appeared to be a man with a lot on his mind. He knew the engagement and wedding probably had a lot to do with it. But for some strange reason, he had a gut feeling the biggest "thing" distracting Ty had to do with a woman. And Grant intended to find out what—or who—it was about.

He was going in blind, but he figured New Year's Eve was a good place to start. "Heard about your New Year's Eve." Ty's expression gave him away. His eyes widened and his brows arched in surprise. *Bingo.*

"What're you talking about? Nobody saw us k—"

"Ah-hah! Now we're gettin' somewhere! Who'd you kiss?"

Ty furrowed his brow. "I'm not talking about this—it was *nothing*", he stated firmly.

Putting his hands up in surrender, Grant smirked, knowing he'd hit the bull's-eye. "Sure. Alright. It was nothing."

Okay, it was something—*she was something*. Kendall Porter had snagged his attention several months earlier at his annual Halloween party. She'd arrived in a short, snug nurse costume. He remembered opening his front door, thoroughly stupefied over how gorgeous she was. At that moment he realized that Kendall Porter—the same little girl that used to spend the night with Olivia when they were younger—had transformed into a beautiful woman.

His eyes had perused her long, lean body. White thigh-high's covered her mile-long legs, fastened to the exposed garters peeking below the hem of her short dress. The mini-dress hugged every subtle curve and the zipper had been left open just enough to expose a hint of cleavage. A red stethoscope hung loosely around her neck—ironic since he heard the roar of his rapid pulse throbbing in his ears. Her lips were layered in a sensual shade of red lipstick, enhancing said lips when she smiled back at him.

That was the first time he'd been tempted by a woman since his split with his estranged wife, Cameron.

Lust had slammed into him like a freight train. In fact, that sensation seemed to happen a lot around Kendall.

"Nothing, huh?" Grant punctuated. "You sure you don't want to change your story?—you've been staring into space for the past five minutes with a foolish fucking grin on your face!"

He was so busted.

And the crux of it: his countless attempts to shake-off that flutter in his gut only seemed to further magnify the sensation.

His marriage was over—had been for a long time. Maybe it was finally time to make it official.

Chapter 2

Opening the locked bottom drawer of his home office desk, Ty removed the divorce papers he'd been served roughly three months earlier. He skimmed through the jargon on each page, thankful Cameron hadn't asked for a portion of his personal belongings or alimony.

He thought back to the first day they'd met. He'd been at the local saloon, watching a Braves' game with some of the guys from the department. After paying his tab, he'd opened the door and witnessed Cameron fall. She'd been walking along the boardwalk in a pair of flesh-colored stilettos and had somehow managed to get the pointed heel wedged between two boards. Her knees buckled and as her body tumbled to the ground, she'd twisted her ankle.

It'd happened so fast. He rushed toward her, but by the time he reached her side the damage had already been done. He assisted her to her feet, instructing her to grab hold of his shoulders while he dislodged her shoe. And once she was free, he'd gazed into her midnight-blue eyes and knew from that very moment that she would be his wife.

They had no business getting married—they'd barely known one another. But she was so beautiful—so captivating—he'd actually convinced himself that it could work. After spending his young adult life raising his little sister, always being the responsible one, he did something completely out of character: he'd thrown caution to the wind, ignored rationale. And three short weeks later, they'd stood at the local courthouse and recited their vows in a civil marriage ceremony.

The first year had been amazing. Sure, they'd had their disagreements from time to time, but they'd had so much fun. They'd went at it like jackrabbits almost daily. Laughed together often. But after the first year, reality sunk in, and ever so slowly, they began drifting apart.

He now realized that he'd never really been in love with Cameron—he'd been in lust. No doubt about it, she was beautiful: average height, a killer body, long blond hair, and some of the nicest medically-enhanced tits he'd ever had the pleasure of seeing. But that kind of physical attraction couldn't sustain a marriage. It was bound to fail—he was just pissed off that it ended the way it did.

She'd had an affair with a successful entre-preneur in town for the annual Oyster Festival last fall. Ty had come home after a long night at the fire station to find her wedding ring lying on the bed they'd shared, along with a farewell letter confessing her dirty deeds...

So much had changed in his life over the last few months and it was about damn time he accepted it and moved forward.

Uncapping his pen, he signed his name on the divorce document, unprepared for the immediate release of tension he'd shouldered for so long. It was finally over. He was a free man again.

It was time to start thinking about what lay ahead. Important things. Like the engagement party he was throwing for Grant and Olivia this weekend.

And the very beautiful maid of honor...

Seventeen days into the first month of the year and Kendall had yet to hear from Ty (not that she was counting or anything). God, she felt so embarrassed—so stupid. She still couldn't believe she revealed he was her "fantasy guy."

And she still couldn't believe how incredibly delicious that kiss had been...

Shaking her head a bit, she forced the memory aside as she sifted through her closet. Tonight was Olivia and Grant's engagement party. She attempted to convince herself that tonight was like any other night. But honestly, who was she fooling? It *was* a big deal—the first time she would see Ty since their kiss a few weeks ago. She prayed it wouldn't be awkward. Maybe if she avoided him tonight, she'd save herself the embarrassment.

Yeah, right... Ty was Grant's best man, and most importantly, the party was being held at his home. Sort of made it next to impossible to keep her distance when he was the host.

She finally settled on a black satin shift dress that showcased her biggest asset: her mile-long legs. She straightened her shoulder-length black hair and added a touch of make-up. And just in case her long, lean legs didn't capture his attention, she opted to enhance her pouty lips with a cherry gloss. Studying her reflection in the full-length mirror, she gave a firm nod. "Huh, take *that* Lieutenant Everitt", she mumbled. "Let's see how unforgettable I am tonight."

How the hell had this happened, exactly? Ty had grabbed several logs from the large stack of wood he kept by Olivia's darkroom out back and somehow managed to get caught by Chief Handler's wife, Debbie. "*Chatty Debbie*", as she was often referred as. She really was a nice lady, but she was also well-known for striking conversations about the most random and oddest of topics. And apparently tonight was no exception.

"Anyone ever tell you that you look like that guy from that street racing movie?"

"*The Fast and the Furious*?" Ty questioned.

"Uh-huh. I saw it for the first time last month and the minute I saw that guy, I thought of you!" She remarked as she gestured with her index finger.

"You mean the big muscular one?" he asked with a wink.

"No—not him—the cute blond one."

Nodding, he sighed. "Yeah, unfortunately, I hear that a lot. When the movie came out the guys at the station had a ball with it." Ty's forehead wrinkled in confusion. Was he really having this conversation with Chief's wife? "I didn't figure you for a street racing fan—no offense."

"Well, that's a correct assumption! You see, my niece, Tina, brought the movie over. She'd been datin' this racecar driver at the time and..."

And that's when he saw her. Sin in a little black

dress: Kendall.

His eyes widened. His jaw became slack. His mouth watered.

"...and walked in and caught the man bitin' his toenails!" Debbie cupped her hand around her mouth and lowered her voice for emphasis. "Apparently he was a flexible lil' fella: got caught red-handed with his big toe in his mouth! I mean, can *you imagine?*"

Son of a bitch!

"But I guess it sort of explains how he chipped that front tooth..."

He watched in amazement as Kendall's eyes skimmed the crowded patio, briefly landing on him before zeroing in on a group of firefighter wives huddled around the poor-excuse-of-a-fire.

"...You know, they say walkin' barefoot is good for you now—but don't go runnin' back tellin' Chief that. I'd hate to give up my shoe collection!"

"That would be terrible. And don't worry, your secret's safe with me", he assured her as he winked again. "Excuse me, will you?—there's a crowd of pretty ladies over there huddled around the fire. And I have the wood", he uttered as he raised the logs in his grip.

Boy did he have wood. One look at Kendall in that little black dress and a certain appendage began to resemble the solid Live Oak he stood underneath.

"Hey ladies", he greeted as he carefully placed the logs in the fire pit. Everyone acknowledged him with a "hello"—all except for Kendall. He couldn't help but notice how her eyes remained on the growing fire; how her fingers nervously tucked a strand of hair behind her ear.

"It should start to warm up in a minute", he reiterated.

He was staring at her. She could see it in her peripheral vision. Could almost feel his heated gaze sear her flesh.

Was she going to avoid eye contact all night? He wondered. Deciding he wasn't going to allow that to happen, he reached toward her, cupping her elbow. "Can I steal you away for a sec?—official best man, maid of honor business."

As soon as those golden peepers landed on him, he nearly lost his breath. They were the color of whiskey and if he wasn't careful, he'd find himself nearly drunk from her gaze.

"Um... sure. Okay."

Placing his hand along the small of her back, he guided her through the crowd and rounded the corner to the side of the house for privacy. "So how've you been?" he asked as they came to a halt.

Kendall turned to face him, rubbing her bare arms for warmth. "Great—if you don't take into account that it's freezing outside tonight. I still can't believe it was seventy degrees last night and now we're on the verge of a freeze warning." She tried to appear casual—at ease—but when his eyes scanned her body like they were doing right now, she couldn't help but feel a surge of excitement.

"You know, that dress is probably illegal in at least half the counties in the state."

Kendall leaned her backside against the side of the house and smiled. "Ah, you noticed."

Scratching the back of his head, his eyes continued their journey. "Hard not to." There was a long stretch of silence as his focus finally settled on her beautiful face. Time to acknowledge the eight-hundred pound gorilla. "Listen, um... I guess we should talk about New Year's—"

"What's there to discuss?" She shrugged non-chalantly. "It was just a New Year's kiss. I guess you were just at the wrong place at the right time."

Taking a step forward, he placed one of his hands along the wall beside her head, satisfied with the sudden intake of breath she inhaled as he moved closer. "What about now?"

"What about it?" she asked, a little more breath-less than she'd intended.

Unable to resist, Ty ran the back of his fingers along her cheek with his free hand. "Does *this* time seem right to you?" His focus was temporarily di-verted to her mouth as she licked her voluptuous cherry lips. He wanted to taste them in the worst way. Wanted to run his tongue along the seam until she opened for him. Wanted to smear that red gloss with his mouth. Wanted to—

"I don't normally kiss married men. And so in *this* case, I'd say your timing is a bit off."

Before he had an opportunity to explain that she'd had it all wrong—that he was, in fact, divorced—she ducked underneath his arm and headed back to the patio. He called out to her as she walked away, but she either didn't hear him or wasn't interested in what he had to say.

He wanted to believe it was the former. Because there was no mistaking the desire behind those per-ceptible golden eyes. She'd wanted him to kiss her—no doubt about it. He'd give her some space—time for the anticipation to build—and then he'd explain that his marriage to Cameron was in the past.

And hopefully, another incredible kiss with the lovely Kendall Porter was in the near future.

* * * * *

They'd almost kissed. Again.

She'd been tempted a little—okay, so she'd been tempted a lot. Her lips tingled at the thought of kissing Ty again. But then reality assaulted her: he was still a married man. A man who hadn't quite accepted that his marriage was over. Or had he?

Damn it, Kendall was so confused. She tried to convince herself that it didn't matter. She wasn't a home wrecker or *the other woman*. Cameron had managed to wreck her marriage all by herself—she'd cheated; she'd filed for divorce.

It'd been roughly three months since he'd been served with the divorce documents, and according to Olivia, had yet to sign them. Obviously he hadn't come to terms. And obviously, Kendall needed to accept the inevitable: pursuing anything other than friendship with Ty would only cause further mental anguish and embarrassment on her part.

"You okay?" Olivia asked as she joined her by the fire.

"Of course, I am!—why do you ask?"

"Well, you're glarin' at the fire with some of the coldest looks I've ever seen. I'm actually sort of surprised you haven't smothered the flames with that icy stare of yours!" Olivia teased as she bumped Kendall shoulder.

Kendall sighed as she spoke, "I'm fine. Really."

"Uh-huh, and you're a terrible liar, too."

That caused Kendall's mouth to turn upward in a smile. Olivia could always sense when she was being—ahem—less than truthful. "I guess that's a good quality to have in a best friend. Isn't it?"

"Totally", Olivia agreed as she stared suspiciously. "Okay—spill it. What's goin' on with you?"

Kendall shook her head. "It's no big deal. Honest.

And besides, this is your engagement party! You need to be focusing all your attention on that handsome man stalking this way toward you."

The two turned their heads and watched as Grant moved closer, an unmistakable expression of bliss on his face as his eyes connected with Olivia.

"There you are—I've been looking for you." Grant tugged on Olivia's waist and pulled her against him, burying his face in the crook of her neck.

"I was only gone for like ten minutes."

Spreading soft kisses along her neck, Grant groaned. "Mmm, it was too long. Missed you."

For heaven's sake, Kendall wanted that. Wanted a man who'd miss her after ten minutes apart—not in a creepy, stalker way—but in a there's-no-one-I'd-rather-spend-my-free-time-with-than-you kind of way.

Olivia had found that with Grant. And she was so incredibly happy for her best friend. She truly was. That kind of love and adoration was rare. And seeing it firsthand only further emphasized to Kendall how far out of reach it was for herself.

Tearing her eyes away from the two lovebirds beside her, Kendall's eyes traversed the patio. There were at least thirty-five people present and maybe a handful were single men.

Those weren't exactly good odds.

Her eye's finally settled on a tall, handsome blond with the magnetic green eyes—green eyes that were currently staring back at her.

Ty.

She wanted someone special in her life. Wanted that someone to be him.

But she refused to be any man's rebound—even if the man in question was her fantasy guy.

Chapter 3

Monday's at the pharmacy reminded Kendall of the movie *Forest Gump*. Because Monday's were like a box of chocolates: she never knew what she was going to get. Sometimes she'd be so busy, she'd work straight though lunch, barely aware that her stomach was practically gnawing on her backbone. And sometimes she'd find herself falling victim to her self-diagnosed OCD, meticulously straightening her work area so that everything was in its preferred place.

Today was an OCD kind of day.

She'd already alphabetized the bags of prescriptions awaiting pick up, making sure to file them back in the basket neatly. She'd wandered down the aisles of shelves behind the counter and made certain all drug labels were facing the correct direction. And now, she was color-coordinating the large collection of highlighters in her top drawer from lightest to darkest.

She really needed to get a life...

Porter Pharmacy was a staple in this small community. Her father had opened it several years before she was born. In fact, some of her earliest memories revolved around this place. She thought back to her childhood, reminiscing about the countless afternoons she'd spent here. She remembered riding her bike here after school every day, sitting behind the pharmacy counter, sipping on a chocolate milkshake. She'd watch her dad consult with customers about possible drug contraindications and council them on everything from which over-the-counter cold medicine would best soothe their symptoms to which pregnancy test garnered the earliest response.

He'd certainly served his community well.

And she'd wanted to be just like him.

After high school, she'd went off to college, following in her father's footsteps by becoming a pharmacist as well. Upon graduation, she'd interviewed with a large chain pharmacy—was days away from being offered the position—when her mother had called with devastating news: her father had suffered a stroke.

That phone call changed everything.

One month after graduation, she traveled back to Butler Island to run the pharmacy her father built. Two years later, she was still here... Waiting for the life she'd painstakingly planned to begin.

"How's the town's prettiest pharmacist doing today?" Ty asked as he leaned his forearms on the counter.

Emerging from her nostalgic trance, Kendall met his spellbinding gaze and tried to ignore the electric jolt that zipped down her spine at the sight of him. "Prettiest?" she questioned as she smiled.

"Most definitely."

"Well, I think you're forgetting I'm the *only* pharmacist in town, which means: no competition."

"There is 'no competition' when it comes to you..."

His statement hung between them for a few moments.

Unbelievable. Simply unbelievable. Just an ordinary compliment and her knees suddenly felt weak. Tucking her hair behind her ear, she cleared her throat in an attempt to regain her composure. "So, what can I do for you?"

"Well, you could start by having dinner with me tonight."

"You're married, remember?"

Ty exposed a sexy grin. "And what if I told you my marriage was officially over?"

"In that case, I'd say... it would have to depend."

"On...?"

"If it was a hypothetical question or the truth", she explained.

Before Ty had the opportunity to disclose his newly-single status, a customer approached from behind.

"Good evening, Kendall", Mr. Mitchell announced before succumbing to a vicious cough attack.

"Oh, Mr. Mitchell—that cough sounds terrible! Would you like a cup of water?" She offered.

The elderly man shook his head and managed to say, "Just my prescription", in between coughs.

Ty backed away from the counter, allowing Kendall the opportunity to consult Mr. Mitchell on his prescription. Meandering through the small store, he picked a random aisle to wander down. Just so happens it was the condom aisle. How ironic...

Had it really been that long since he'd needed items from this particular aisle? Yes, it most certainly had. He couldn't believe some of the things he was seeing: his and her lubricants that promised increased sensitivity and explosive results, cock rings, and vibrators disguised and marketed as *female massagers.*

He wondered how many Butler Island residents actually bought some of these items. And if a certain beautiful pharmacist owned any of them...

But he didn't have to wonder long, because a loud gasp from the back of the store suddenly halted his brief reverie.

"Now remember, make sure you take this medication with food. Otherwise, you'll run the risk of getting an upset stomach on top of all the other symptoms you're experiencing", Kendall explained as she handed Mr. Mitchell his prescription.

"Will do. Thanks, darlin'."

"You're welcome."

After Mr. Mitchell turned to exit the pharmacy, Kendall knelt down and opened her bottom drawer. She searched for the small container of hand sanitizer she kept to prevent the spread of germs she often came into contact with whenever she assisted sick patients, and quickly rubbed it in. Her latest customer had a rather bad case of the flu and she couldn't afford to close the pharmacy for a few days in the event she were to catch it too.

She was aware of the jingle that sounded when the door to the pharmacy opened. Unsure if it was Mr. Mitchell leaving, or another customer arriving, she quickly tossed the hand sanitizer back into the bottom drawer and stood up. Only when she rose from behind the counter did she realize it wasn't a customer.

Like a reflex, she gasped at the two people

standing in front of her on the opposite side of the counter: two masked men, one tall and broad, one short and slender.

And both aiming guns at her.

Kendall threw her hands up in front of her in surrender. "We d-don't keep a lot of money here", she stuttered. "We mostly d-deal in insurance, b-but everything we do have is yours—"

"Thanks for the offer", the tall masked-man interrupted, "but you have something far more valuable than what's in your register..."

His eyes had to be playing tricks on him, because as Ty peeked around the corner of the aisle, he saw two men in masks pointing guns toward Kendall. *Holy shit!*

He had to do something—had to take their attention away from her. He plotted for a quick moment. One of the masked-men was tall and looked to be in pretty good shape, but the other one was much smaller. The short one wore baggy clothes, but Ty could still tell the little gunman had a small frame. He could easily take him out with little to no effort—probably could take the bigger one easily as well—but he didn't want to risk Kendall's safety.

He stole a quick glance at Kendall. God, she was scared—and rightfully so. Ty knew he had only one option in order to keep her safe: make his presence known. Raising his hands in front of him, he emerged from the aisle. "Everything okay?"

"Ty!" Kendall shrieked as he took a step toward her.

The large intruder immediately turned his gun

on Ty. "Stop right there", he warned. "Take another step and the pretty pharmacist's brain matter will be splatter on the wall before you'd even be able to reach the counter. You want that on your conscience?"

Ty forced his eyes to move toward Kendall again. Damn it, she was pale and her bottom lip was trembling. She was absolutely terrified.

And so was he.

But the last thing he'd do was put her in any more danger than they were already in. Ty locked eyes with the large gunman. "No. I don't want anyone to get hurt."

"Good answer", the large gunman replied. And without taking his eyes off Ty, he explained what he wanted. "Here's what's going to happen: the pretty pharmacist is going to fill a very large prescription today. I have three bags: the first one is going to be filled with Oxycontin. The second: Vicodin. And last, but certainly not least, the third bag: Xanax. And to ensure we aren't cheated, my partner is going to accompany the pharmacist behind the counter with the gun. Are we clear?"

"Y-yes", Kendall sputtered.

Ty gave a firm nod in understanding and watched as the small gunman opened the half-door to gain access to Kendall and the drugs behind the counter.

Kendall pivoted toward the shelves that stocked the three drugs the men requested and gasped when she felt the muzzle of the handgun jar against her spine. Each step she took was more frightening than the last. Her knees wobbled, threatening to collapse beneath her.

Finally they came upon the aisle that housed the pharmacy's supply of controlled substances. The small gunman tossed the first bag at her and motioned for Kendall to empty the pills into it. Her hands shook wildly as she poured the Oxycontin into the first bag. She concentrated on slowing her breathing, knowing if she made the mistake of dropping the pills, she'd risk becoming injured. Or worse...

After the first bag was filled, she repeated the same process with the remaining drugs and then returned to the counter.

"Nice job", the large gunman praised. "Now place the bags on the counter. Slowly." He waited for her to comply and then gestured toward Ty. "You. Get behind the counter with the pretty lady."

Making sure to keep his hands in clear sight, Ty walked toward the half-door and stood next to Kendall.

The unadulterated fear in her eyes nearly severed his heart in two. He'd die before he'd let anything happen to her. He wanted to reassure her. Needed for her to know that he'd protect her.

"Now we're going to take a little walk to the back office", the big gunman announced.

Ty and Kendall turned their backs to the gunmen and began walking toward the back corner where her office was located.

In his peripheral vision, Ty watched as Kendall bit her bottom lip in an attempt to suppress a fleeing sob. "It's almost over, Doll", he whispered softly. "You're doing great—"

"No talking!"

When they arrived at her office, the big masked-man motioned for Ty to enter first. He hesitated for a moment, afraid the men would lock him inside and do Lord knows what with Kendall, but quickly stepped

forward when the muzzle of one of the guns pressed
into the back of his skull. "Please, don't hurt her", he
managed calmly. "She did everything you asked."

"Shut up and get inside", the large intruder
instructed as he nudged Ty through the doorway.

Once inside, Ty pivoted to face the door and
witnessed the small man forcibly shove Kendall into
the small room. The fucking coward shoved her with
such fury, she stumbled and fell to the floor beside
his feet.

Instinctively, Ty started toward her. But the
large gunman took a step forward and aimed the gun
at Ty's forehead.

"Don't move!" he shouted angrily.

Ty remained idle as the small man unplugged
the phone on Kendall's desk and took it with him as
he exited the tiny room.

"It sure was a pleasure doing business with you",
the large man proclaimed as he stepped backwards
out of the room.

Ty remained still until the door slammed shut
and then lunged to the floor toward Kendall. "You
alright?"

Kendall quickly nodded and then let out another
sob.

"Are you hurt?"

"Just my wrist."

"Let me see", Ty uttered as he carefully inspected her wrist. "Could be broken."

Kendall inhaled a shaky breath. "Great", she
murmured sarcastically. "Do you think they're g-gone
now?"

Ty stood up and walked toward the door. He
tried the knob: it turned, but the door wouldn't budge.
"Looks like they wedged the door shut."

"How're we gonna get help, then? They took the phone on my desk and my cell phone's in the bottom drawer at the counter."

Reaching into his back pocket, Ty gripped his Blackberry. "Lucky for us, I still have mine."

Chapter 4

It wasn't long before the police arrived, freeing them from Kendall's office. The door had been fixed with a two-by-six board, positioned just underneath the doorknob and wedged against one of the shelves that housed psychiatric medications—believe it or not.

The next hour was a blur as detectives carefully scoured the pharmacy for evidence. Of course, there was none. The gunmen were wearing masks to disguise their identities and gloves to prevent the transfer of their fingerprints. Kendall was questioned repeatedly about how the robbery unfolded, as was Ty, and when the detectives felt they'd thoroughly pieced together what little information was available, the police announced the two were free to go.

"How's the wrist?" Ty questioned as he ambled toward her.

"It still hurts. Although considering I had a gun pointed at me a little over an hour ago, I'd say it's pretty minor."

Ty studied her for a moment. She was trying so

hard to hold herself together, but underneath that cool façade, he sensed she was in a lot of pain. "We need to get you to the hospital for an x-ray."

"Kendall shook her head. "I'm fine—*really*. There's no need to—"

"No", he stated firmly. "We're gonna get it checked out. Now."

Kendall opened her mouth to say something and then quickly closed it. She returned Ty's intense glare, unable to overlook how tightly his jaw was clenched. Obviously, he wasn't going to budge on the x-ray thing. And truthfully she was too exhausted to argue with him. "Alright", she conceded, "let me just grab my purse."

The trip to the hospital had turned out to be a good move. The x-ray revealed her wrist wasn't broken, only sprained. At least something was going her way tonight, she thought wryly. Although she couldn't help but wonder if her eventful evening was karma's way of leveling the score (she had kissed a married man on New Year's Eve, after all).

The sun had long set by the time Ty man-euvered his large truck into her driveway.

"Are you sure you don't want me to take you back by the pharmacy to get your car?—I don't mind."

"No. I spoke to Marcus when I was waiting to hear the x-ray results. He said he'd swing by in the morning. I can ride with him." Marcus was her phar-macy assistant—her right hand man (*her very short, right hand man*). He'd worked at the pharmacy for years and had been a tremendous help when she'd first taken her father's place two years ago. He'd been scheduled to work that evening with her until they closed, but because business had been particularly slow, she'd given him the rest of the afternoon off.

Nodding his head, Ty shoved the gear into park and then turned his head toward her. "You know, if you were looking for an excuse to get out of having dinner with me tonight, this was a little extreme."

At that moment, Kendall laughed—*really laughed.* He loved hearing it. Loved how the worrisome look faded from her angelic face.

"Well, I don't have much in my fridge—haven't been to the grocery store in a while—but we could order pizza from Bruno's", she offered.

"There's nothing quite like eating a pizza with a beautiful lady after an armed robbery", he stated with a wide grin.

Kendall laughed again. "Well, then, c'mon."

Ty assisted her out of the truck and then followed her up the front porch steps. Once inside the pale yellow Craftsman bungalow, she gave him a quick tour.

The inside was rather small, but comfortable. Cozy. The living room opened to the kitchen, separated by a small breakfast bar, giving the modest bungalow an open, airy aura. The décor was without a doubt a reflection of Kendall's style: simple elegance with just the right amount of femininity, enabling even the most manliest of men to feel comfortable.

Manliest of men? The sudden realization that Kendall had entertained other men in her home caused an unexpected pang of jealousy. Wow. He was completely unprepared for that... Of course other men had probably been here—he wasn't naive. Knew she'd dated from time to time, although nothing serious (and from what he understood, nothing *recent*). Forcing the discovery aside he gestured toward the wood staircase. "What's up there?"

"Just a bathroom and a small loft—*my room.* The other bedroom is on the first floor, down the hall on the right."

"This is nice—I like it here", he stated as he followed her into the kitchen.

"Thanks. I like it here, too—it kind of feels like an escape after a long day at the pharmacy", she said as she gestured for him to take a seat at the breakfast bar.

"Well, I can see why."

Kendall opened the drawer next to the fridge where she kept her take out menus and quickly thumbed through the small stack until she came upon the menu for Bruno's Italian Kitchen. She tossed the cardstock menu toward him as though she were launching a Frisbee, impressed with his quick reflexes when he caught it with one hand. "You mind calling in the order?" she asked. "I'd really like to jump in the shower before we eat."

*Oh boy...*Without warning, Ty's mind was invaded with images of Kendall standing underneath the showerhead, her hair dripping wet, rivulets of water cascading down her sleek, naked body...

"Ty...?"

"Huh?"

"Is pizza okay?—I mean we can order something else if—"

"No. Pizza sounds perfect... What toppings do you like?" He asked as he internally scolded himself for having x-rated thoughts of Kendall in the shower.

"I'm not picky—just make sure there's no anchovies. I hate those things."

"One extra-anchovy pizza coming right up." Kendall shot him a playful scowl as she crossed her arms. "Okay, okay", he amended as he put his hands up. "Don't worry. I'll take care of it!"

Satisfied, Kendall smiled and then turned toward the wood staircase. Ty's gaze fell upon her back and then promptly targeted her swaying hips as she retreated. The black pencil skirt did dangerous things to her perfectly round ass (and obvious things to his family jewels).

Fuck! He really needed to get a grip. And quickly.

Wiping one of his hands down his face, he glanced at the menu and then reached for his Blackberry. Once the order was called in, he stood from the stool and walked to the fridge. He chuckled softly to himself; she wasn't kidding when she mentioned she hadn't been grocery shopping in a while. The shelves were noticeably bare, but she did have the perfect accompaniment to any pizza dish: beer.

Funny how most single folks could procrastinate when it came to stocking their refrigerators with food, but never forgot to replenish their supply of alcohol. He snagged two Heineken's from the perfectly aligned rows and removed the caps.

He set the bottles on the breakfast bar and then peeked into several of her kitchen cupboards in search of plates. Finding them in the cabinet next to the stove, he reached inside and heard a subtle creak from the hardwood floors as Kendall rejoined him in the kitchen. "Hope you don't mind", he called out as he gripped two dinner plates. "I went ahead and set— *holy shit!*" He exclaimed as he turned to face her.

Kendall was wearing an old, heather-gray college sweatshirt—only it'd been modified: *Flashdance* rem-

iniscent. She'd cut the sleeves and made the neckline
wider, causing the soft material to shift, revealing
one of her bare shoulders. She paired it with short,
navy satin boxers that showcased her mile-long legs.

Sweet baby Jesus, he was in big trouble...

Ty was unsure how long he'd been standing
with the plates in his hands, staring at the flawless
form leaning against the small column next to the
breakfast bar. It must have been a considerable
amount of time, because when Kendall finally spoke,
her tone was one that echoed amusement.

"Simon says: stop staring at me like that."

"Trust me, Simon wouldn't say that if he had
my perspective..."

Their eyes met and held for several intense
seconds before she finally broke the silence. "Thank
you for setting up", she said, realizing that a subject
change was well overdue.

Ty stepped forward and placed the plates on the
bar. "You're welcome." With his hands now free, he
picked up the Heinekens and handed one to her.
"Figured after the day we had, we needed these."

"Thanks." They each raised the bottles to their
lips and took a long pull, eyes never swaying from
the other.

As if on cue, the doorbell rang, interrupting
their sensual trance.

"I should probably get that", she uttered softly.

"Huh-uh. Sit down. My treat tonight..." The
doorbell rang again as Ty set his beer on the bar. "Be
right back."

Kendall sat on one of the stools, thankful she
didn't have to walk far to get to it. Her knees felt
wobbly and this time it had nothing to do with being
robbed at gunpoint.

Ty returned moments later carrying a plastic bag filled with several Styrofoam containers. She watched as he opened one of the containers and removed two gigantic slices of pizza, carefully placing them on their awaiting plates.

"I'm curious... Did any of your—ahem—*fantasies* include me serving you dinner?" He asked as he uncovered a suggestive grin.

"Omigod!" Kendall cried as she buried her face in her hands. "I was *really* hoping you were too drunk to remember that!"

Ty chuckled softly as he sat down beside her. Wasn't every day the confident Kendall Porter became timid and embarrassed. "Not a chance", he assured her. "But I do have one more question, though." Reaching for her hands, he peeled them away from her face.

"Okay—shoot", she answered on a sigh.

Taking a bite of his pizza, Ty chewed before asking, "Did kissing me live up to your expectations?"

Oh boy. "Wouldn't you like to know..."

Ty took another bite. "Yeah, I would, actually."

"On a fishing expedition, are you?"

"Maybe..."

Kendall shrugged nonchalantly. "Well, I'm sorry—guess you're outta luck. I *never* kiss and tell..." She smiled at him before taking a bite of her slice.

He liked verbally sparring with her—liked how playful they were toward one another. "That bad, huh?"

Kendall met his curious gaze and smiled. "I don't think you have anything to worry about."

"Ah-hah", he uttered as he pointed with his index finger. "So you liked it just as much as I did."

She wasn't going there. Lowering her head, she

looked down at her lap and smiled, tucking her still damp hair behind her ear. "So what else is in the bag?"

Ty turned his attention toward the bag and then back to Kendall. "Dessert." Rising from the stool, he walked several paces to the nearby counter and removed a small Styrofoam container from the bag, along with a plastic fork. Retracing his steps, he returned to his stool and opened the lid as he placed it between them on the bar. "Hope you still like tiramisu."

Smiling, she answered, "It's one of my favorites."

"I remember... Every time you came with me and Liv to Bruno's for dinner, you'd always order tiramisu for dessert..."

Kendall was rendered speechless—a rare phenomenon she didn't experience often. One thing her friends could always count on was her ability to voice her opinion (even when she wasn't asked for her contribution). She tried not to read too much into it. So he remembered how much she liked tiramisu— half the island knew that. Just one example of the downside of living in a small town.

But the thing was: it *did* matter. His dessert choice mattered more than it should have and left her wondering if the look in his eyes at that moment meant that she mattered to him, too.

She hadn't uttered a word, but she didn't need to; the expression on her face and the enamored look in her caramel eyes told him everything he needed to know. Ty picked up the fork, speared a portion off the edge, and then held it out for her. "Simon says: open wide."

Kendall complied, opening her luscious mouth. Ty placed the espresso-flavored dessert on her tongue and swallowed a groan as her voluptuous, rose lips clamped down around the plastic fork. Her large almond-shaped eyes closed, savoring the creamy decadence on her tongue. And when he slid the fork from her lips, a delicious moan escaped from the back of her throat. The sound reverberated through his body, sending a white-hot ball of lust to his groin.

When she finally opened her eyes, Ty was staring at her, wicked intentions in his lust-filled gaze. Kendall licked her lips after swallowing the velvety treat. "Tastes like heaven", she stated softly.

Grinning, Ty stabbed the plastic fork into the dessert and then inched forward. "Guess it's my turn to take a taste, then." He could care less about the tiramisu, he wanted to taste her again.

When his mouth was but a whisper away, her lips parted, and then… *sweet heaven*. He savored her mouth like he was tasting a fine wine: slowly swirling his tongue to capture her essence on all of his taste buds. He relished the sweetness, treasured each stroke of her tongue, and took great pleasure in their gentle, steady rhythm.

Kendall could feel her body melting—liquefying— with every soft collision of his tongue. The New Year's kiss had been incredible—but this kiss? Well… there were no words to describe how amazing it was. Otherworldly: that was the best she could come up with. Because she suspected no other man in the world could choreograph a kiss quite like this man.

And then reality struck (gosh, she hated when that happened). Coming to her senses, Kendall gently shoved his chest, temporarily interrupting their mating mouths. "What are we doing?" she whispered.

"Having dessert." His mouth came over hers again for a second sampling of creamy tiramisu and sinfully sweet Kendall.

She couldn't help herself: she gave in to the kiss. She allowed herself a few blissful moments and then pulled away. "I'm serious."

"So am I", he countered gravelly.

Kendall stared into his Peridot-colored eyes, noticing the small flecks of gold floating in their depths for the very first time. They were glazed with lust and she couldn't deny the shiver of excitement: she was responsible for the wantonness in his gaze. "You're still married, Ty. And even though yours is a unique set of circumstances, the truth is—"

"I'm not married anymore—"

"—this is wrong. I know it sounds crazy, but I feel like a homewrecker—"

"You're not a homewrecker. My marriage is over—"

"—I have a conscience and even though—wait... what did you just say?" She questioned.

"My marriage is over. I signed the divorce papers—last week, in fact..."

Kendall eyed him. "Okaaay", she uttered cautiously.

"Why do I get the feeling that pretty little mind of yours is working overtime to come up with another excuse?"

Maybe because she was. Don't get her wrong, she wanted Ty—had for years. But, well, it was complicated. "Look, I'm..."

"Beautiful", he said matter-of-factly as he brushed a segment of hair away from her eye. "You're beautiful. Smart. Fun to be with... I like you, Kendall."

"Ditto", she whispered.

"I was hoping you'd say that", he commented as he winked. He reached for her hand when she smiled and then began to reveal what he wanted. "I'm not in any position to make any promises, but I do like you, Kendall. A lot... Let's just... take things one day at a time. See where this leads... See if reality is better than those fantasies of yours."

Kendall shoved him playfully and smiled. "You're never gonna let me forget that, are you?"

"Never", he answered while exposing a sexy grin.

"Yeah. Didn't think so..." When the same segment of hair fell around her eye again, his fingertips swept across her cheek and tucked the strands behind her ear. It was a platonic gesture, but somehow it felt like more. Every time he touched her it felt sensual. Purposeful.

Perilous.

"Well, listen", she began, "I think we should call it a night. It's been a long day and I have an even longer one ahead of me tomorrow."

"You sure? Because I could stay", he suggested. Kendall raised one of her eyebrows. "On the couch, of course. Geez, Kendall—rushing those fantasies of yours already, are you?" He watched as she opened her mouth to say something, only to close it moments later.

How on earth had he managed to do that again?—render her speechless...

"I'm only kidding with you", he revealed as he stood from his stool. He picked up his empty plate and the Heineken and trekked into the kitchen. After throwing the bottle in the trash, he gently sat the plate in the sink.

"Wanna take the last slice of pizza with you?" she offered.

"No thanks. " Judging by the near empty fridge,

she needed that extra slice far more than he did.

"I'll walk you out."

Ty followed her to the front door, reminding her to ice her wrist and keep it elevated for the rest of the evening.

"Will do", she conceded as she turned to face him.

"You sure you're gonna be okay here tonight by yourself?"

She had no idea who'd held them at gunpoint. Could have been complete strangers passing through town—at least that's what she wanted to believe. Because if the masked-men lived on the island, chances were good they knew where she lived. That was a bit unsettling... And as disconcerting as that was, she knew Ty sleeping here tonight was far more dangerous.

"Positive."

Tugging on her waist, he nestled her infallible feminine body against his for another devastating kiss, careful not to linger too long—he wanted her hungry for more. Each stroke was meant to lull her and enliven her at the same time. Before pulling away, he suckled on her full bottom lip, satisfied with the breathless sigh that fled her mouth from the erotic sensation. "Mmmm. You're right", he admitted. "Tastes like heaven."

"The tiramisu?"

"Huh-uh... *You.*" He planted a quick kiss on her forehead before opening the front door. "I'll call you tomorrow, Doll."

"Okay", she whispered.

Kendall shut the door and then turned to lean against it. She ran her fingertips over her tingling lips, still wet and swollen from his kiss, and then released a shaky breath.

Oh boy. She was in way over her head.

What on Earth had she been thinking? She'd always had a strong intuition—always trusted the robust inner voice that often whispered forewarnings. And right now, that voice was instructing her to stay clear of Ty. Because Lieutenant Everitt was devilishly dangerous. Sin disguised in a pair of faded blue jeans.

But he'd been completely honest with her: he'd made his divorce final. He was a single man again—free to dive into the dating pool—and what better way to test the water than to take a dip with a sure thing?

Their attraction was mutual, yes, but Ty knew she'd fantasized about him 'for years (an admission she still couldn't believe she'd revealed). What would happen if they finally gave in to their mutual attraction?

Well, that was simple, wasn't it?

He'd get his fill of her—and regain his confidence as an irresistible player, no doubt—and she'd be halfway to falling for him.

Let's just... take things one day at a time. See where this leads, he'd said. A perfect line to utter when one wanted a physical relationship, no emotions involved. Trouble was, she knew where things would lead: down a winding, dead-end road. Ty had just ended his marriage—no way was he ready to make a commitment to her, or anyone else for that matter.

And while she wasn't suggesting he was a contender for the role of her future husband, she wasn't sure she wanted to waste her days pining after a man who may never yearn for the position.

Chapter 5

The following day, Kendall caught a ride with Marcus to the pharmacy. They'd spent a better part of the day cleaning up the mess the police made when they'd combed the place for evidence the evening before. The front of the store looked fine to the naked eye, but her self-diagnosed OCD practically made her fingers twitch with the need to straighten the various over-the-counter products that'd been moved by the detectives.

But that would have to wait. Because the monstrosity behind the pharmacy counter assaulted her self-admitted weakness like a firm slap to the face. Black powder residue used to dust for fingerprints was still visible on much of the surfaces (even though she denoted they wouldn't find any—the men wore gloves), various papers were scattered along the floor, and all of her drawers had been ransacked. So much for the color-coordinated highlighter organization she'd performed yesterday.

Kendall decided to keep the pharmacy closed until just before lunch, allowing her and Marcus a few uninterrupted hours of cleaning time. That decision had paid off. Because when she finally unlocked the front door, a steady trickle of concerned residents dropped in to assess her condition—and collect an earful of firsthand gossip, no doubt.

As the day drew on, it became clear that she needed to invest in a basic security system. Gone were the innocent days of smiling when the bell at the front door jingled. In fact, she now found it next to impossible not to cringe when she heard the familiar sound. She made a mental note to call a few security companies for estimates after she phoned the wholesale distributor that supplied her with the drugs that'd been taken in yesterday's robbery.

The past twenty-four hours still seemed like a bad dream. Her father had opened for business in 1982 and not once had there been a robbery.

Not once.

She wondered what he'd think about yesterday's debacle—what he'd say if he were still able to speak... Deep down she knew it wasn't her fault. But she couldn't help but feel as though she'd failed him somehow.

Just then her cell phone rang, forcing her to re-emerge from her private pity party. She wrestled with herself about whether to answer it. She had a mountain of tasks queuing on her long to-do list and not enough hours left in the drawn out workday to cross half of them off. Besides, her gut told her the call was likely from Ty. He'd left several messages on her voicemail already (guess she'd failed to mention she hadn't been *too busy* to listen to them earlier).

He was concerned about her, relaying that once the shock of what'd happened with the masked-men yesterday wore off, she'd need a friend. *A friend.*

Well, she had plenty of those; didn't need the confusion that accompanied *his* idea of friendship.

Her cell phone quieted, only to be followed by the sound of the pharmacy phone ringing. She hesitated to answer it for a moment, but then suddenly thought better of it. What if the call was a potential customer?

Taking in a hefty liter of air, she picked up the handset and brought it to her ear. "Porter Pharmacy", she greeted in her most pleasant voice.

"Everything alright?"

Oh, she was good—too good. She just knew it was going to be him.

Just. Knew. It.

Honestly, when was she going to ditch this job and put her talented and predictable intuition to good use? People would pay good money to access the kind of information her intuitiveness often provided.

"Are you still there?" Ty continued.

"Yeah, just really busy. Can I call you back later?"

"Yeah... Sure."

Kendall placed the receiver down and exhaled a shaky breath.

There was no use denying she liked him. Always had. But there were extenuating circumstances that kept the yearning cornered deep within. Yes, she was elated—borderline euphoric—that Ty was showing interest in her, ebullient that after years of pining over him, he'd finally noticed her.

But a myriad of other emotions plagued her as well: confusion about his intentions, apprehension about whether he was ready to begin a relationship—and if she was, too. She had serious doubts about whether she could casually take *one-day-at-a-*

time. What would happen when he grew tired of her? He was her best friend's older brother—it's not like she could spend an eternity avoiding him.

She cared so much for him already—probably more than she should—and the last thing she wanted was a permanent awkwardness to settle between them if things didn't end well.

She was becoming far too fond of Lieutenant Everitt. Probably best to douse the growing flames burning between them before the heartbreak he'd inevitably unleash smothered any real chance at a normal, platonic friendship.

Ever since she'd went off to college, she'd dreamt of putting down roots in a sizable city, where what she ordered for lunch wasn't the topic of town gossip. That admission tended to scare away what little decent single men were left in the county— hence why she was twenty-eight and still single.

Crazy as it sounded, she didn't want to be just a warm body in Ty's bed—his first strategic attempt to move on with his life. She wanted more and unfortunately she wasn't in any position to ask for it.

So maybe if she kept her distance, Ty's sudden fascination with her would diminish. And then they both could carry on with their lives. And she could concentrate on attaining her big-city dreams, instead of focusing on the man who'd starred in her fantasies for the last decade.

Ty placed his Blackberry on the kitchen counter and stared at it as if he could will the damn thing to ring again. He'd called Kendall on her cell several times today already, only to be greeted by her voicemail. And when he finally reached her on the pharmacy line, she'd quickly snubbed him with an *"I'm busy"* and a promise that she'd return his call later.

He probably shouldn't read anything into it. Knew she had a lot of loose ends to tie up today. But he couldn't ignore the twist in his gut. Couldn't help but wonder if there was more to it. Because he was getting the inkling that she was deliberately avoiding him.

What was it about Kendall Porter that had him tied up in knots all day?

That was easy: she was beautiful, tenacious, whimsical, confident. And did he mention beautiful?

The vibe he felt last night was that she was trying her damnedest to fend off his advances.

Good thing he was confident and tenacious, too.

Because he wasn't going to give her the opportunity to dismantle what progress they'd already made. It was time to stack the odds in his favor. And he knew just what to do to snag her undivided attention.

Kendall finally made it home just after eight-thirty, feeling nearly dead on her feet. After kicking off her three inch heels, she removed her clothes and slipped on a teal satin robe, loving the way the slippery soft material felt against her tired body. Next on her agenda: dinner.

Shuffling into the kitchen, she opened the fridge.

Empty.

She still hadn't made it to the grocery store. The leftover slice of pizza had been her breakfast this morning and since she'd worked through lunch, the cheesy indulgence was the only source of fuel she'd had all day. After closing the fridge, she stepped toward the pantry and took inventory of her choices: one meager can of tuna, one container of jellied cranberry sauce leftover from Thanksgiving, and a small box of baking soda.

Kendall groaned as her forehead thumped against the pantry door. "Can this day get any worse?" she mumbled.

The sound of the doorbell ringing hauled Kendall from her hunger-induced trance back to reality, and with a cautious gait, she headed toward the front door.

Who'd be dropping by unannounced this late on a Tuesday evening? Aligning her eye with the peephole, she took a gander at the person standing on the other side.

Ty.

Apparently the torture from her hellish day would continue.

Kendall turned the deadbolt, but kept the chain lock fastened. Opening the door as far as the chain allowed, she positioned her face along the gap.

"Hey, Doll", Ty greeted.

"Hey."

"You didn't call me back earlier. I was worried about you."

"Oh, sorry about that. It's been a really hectic day and—"

"You hungry?" Ty interrupted.

"No. Actually, I'm—" At that moment, Kendall's body betrayed her. Her stomach unleashed an angry growl.

Ty arched his brows. "You sure 'bout that?"

"Look", she began on a sigh, "I appreciate your concern, but—"

Ty held up two white bags. "Figured the last thing you'd feel like doin' tonight was cook."

Kendall eyed the two white bags he held in his grip, her mouth literally watering when she discovered the small grease stain in one of the corners. "Whatcha got in those bags?"

Shrugging his shoulders nonchalantly, he answered, "Oh, you know, just a double bacon cheeseburger from the diner." He was using one of her weaknesses against her. Kendall loved good food; never shied away from eating a calorie-packed meal. Just one of the many things he liked about her—she wasn't a *salad-with-the-dressing-on-the-side* kind of girl.

Kendall hesitated for a moment before asking, "Fries or onion rings?"

"Onion rings."

The door suddenly slammed shut, leaving Ty to wonder if he'd made a mistake in choosing her side item. Maybe he should've phoned Olivia. His little sister would've known which of the two choices Kendall preferred. Moments passed before he heard the unmistakable sound of the chain latch sliding from its groove. And then the door opened.

Kendall stood before him wearing a pleasant smile, a small Velcro splint on her injured wrist, and a short silky robe.

Ah, hell...

Kendall motioned for him to come inside, her olfactory sensors alert as she inhaled the greasy goodness wafting in the air. "I'm a sucker for onion rings", she embarrassedly shared after shutting the door behind him.

"Well, then, that makes two of us", he confessed as he followed her to the breakfast bar.

"Id offer you a beer, but I'm all out. I do have a bottle of Cab, though. Do you drink wine?"

"On occasion. I'd love a glass if it's not too much trouble."

"No trouble at all", she responded. "In fact, after the day I had, I could use a glass—or three—to unwind."

Ty took in the view as she rose onto her toes, reaching overhead for the bottle of Cabernet situated in the wine rack above the fridge. He swallowed a groan as the hem of her satin robe ascended up her mile-long legs, settling just beneath the contours of her mighty-fine-looking ass. Heaven help him...

Gripping the neck of the bottle, Kendall gave it a tug, freeing it from its temporary home. She heard the rumpling of the bags opening over her shoulder as she removed the cork, and then plucked two wine glasses from the cupboard. She sat the glasses on the bar and filled each one a little more than half full before joining Ty on the other side.

They sat in comfortable silence until she picked up an onion ring and took her first bite. "Mmmm. It still boggles my mind that a vegetable can taste this good", she rambled. "Onion rings are on my death row last request list. If I'm gonna go, I'm leaving this earth with a belly full of these", she gestured.

Ty laughed. "You have one of those?"

"Sure—don't you?"

"No. Guess I never really thought about it, to tell you the truth."

"You haven't?" she asked incredulously. "Never wondered what delicacy would be digesting in your gut while the executioner pushed a fatal drug cocktail in your veins?"

"Well, considering I never plan to be in that

position to begin with—no."

"Yeah, sure", she started sarcastically, "If you want to look at it *that way*..."

Taking a bite of his onion ring, he thought about it for a moment. "Okay, *hypothetically speaking*", he emphasized, "if I had to choose my last meal, I'd pick nachos—and not the kind with the shredded cheese that hardens by the time they place the platter in front of me. I want the real shit: the gooey cheese that clings to my fingertips."

"Ooh, that's a good one! Maybe if I bat my eyelashes at the guard, he'll give me a side of nachos with my onion rings."

"Let's hope it never comes to that", he shared before taking a bite of his burger.

She watched as he reached for his wine and couldn't help but laugh at their strange fusion menu: All-American bacon cheeseburgers, crispy onion rings, two dill pickle spears, and a pricey bottle of Cabernet Sauvignon.

"What's so funny?" he asked after setting the glass down on the bar.

Kendall gestured toward their glasses. "If a wine sommelier saw us drinking that with our bacon cheeseburgers, they'd probably kick the bucket."

Ty trenched his brows together in confusion. "I thought red wine and beef were supposed to be paired together."

"Filet mignon, sure. But ground chuck smothered with mayo, cheddar cheese, and a heaping pile of crispy bacon?—not so much." The sound of Ty's laughter monopolized the room, echoing off the walls and filling her insides with an overwhelming need to hear it again. "I like hearing you laugh", she confessed as the volume of his cackle quieted.

Turning in the stool to face her, he leaned his elbow against the bar. "I seem to do that a lot when I'm around you. Can't say I've done a whole hell of a lot of laughing these last five months..." Nope. The last five months had been no laughing matter. It'd started with the discovery of Cameron's infidelity and sudden departure. And not long after that, the fires began.

The small town of Butler Island had experienced an uncanny amount of fires last fall, the work of a skilled arsonist. His sister, Olivia, had even been attacked by the son of a bitch twice when she'd captured him setting the boat warehouse ablaze with her camera. Then came the shock: the man responsible had been a fellow firefighter. No, he hadn't had much to smile about then.

But now? Now he was grinning at the woman who was largely responsible for his blissful demeanor these days.

"Well, you should definitely try to do it more often. It looks good on you", Kendall reiterated.

"Thank you."

There was barely a crumb left by the time their hunger was sated. They sat at the breakfast bar facing one another, chatting about various topics, the level of remaining wine in the bottle slowly receding as they took turns refilling their glasses.

As the seconds ticked by, concentration on anything other than the way Kendall looked in her satiny robe became... problematic. Hell, did she not realize what she was doing to him right now? The ends of the material had separated slightly when she'd crossed her legs earlier, exposing a trace of soft skin along one of her thighs. Her manicured hands gripped her wine glass casually, her nails painted to match her toes: candy apple red.

It was strange, really: he'd never thought feet could be... sexy. But something about her bare feet did him in. Lust sucker punched him the moment she'd opened the door tonight. And after three glasses of wine, he was beginning to question why he'd thought it was a good idea to suppress it in the first place.

He longed to examine the hidden treasure underneath her robe. In fact, his fingers practically twitched at the thought of tugging on the satin belt that cinched the material closed—

"You're spoiling me, you know", Kendall admitted.

"How so?"

"Two nights in a row, you've bought dinner. If you're not careful, I may start to expect this on a regular basis." Kendall swirled the remainder of wine in her glass as her eyes trekked along the contours of Ty's unshaven face.

"Hope so..."

The wine had certainly loosened her up a bit, leaving her to question the logic behind her earlier decision to deflect Ty's advances. She placed her glass on the bar and then traced her fingertips along the edge of the rim. "What's on the menu for dessert?"

Ty grinned. "You." The pad of his thumb grazed the surface of her full bottom lip, tugging on the succulent flesh slightly as he inched forward.

Her lips parted as he narrowed the distance between them, and at the very last moment, he palmed the sides of her face, holding her steady while his mouth prepared to land against hers. Kendall's lips were lush. Soft. Like a pillow in the finest five-star presidential suite.

Their tongues met and dueled, each demanding dominance and obedience from the other.

Kendall was fighting for control, battling the need threatening to overwhelm her. The pace was accelerating, the desire for this man overthrowing logic and reason. Because her body knew what it wanted— whom it wanted.

Her hands began roaming, exploring the hardened surface of his chest, itching to get underneath his shirt to feel his heated skin with her fingertips. She could feel the heavy thump of his heart pounding against the palms of her hands, almost beating as fast as hers.

Without warning, Ty ended the kiss. He slid off the stool and caressed her thighs with his large callused hands, positioning her once-crossed legs into the shape of a V so he could stand between them. His eyes pinned her body as they bored into hers, paralyzing her muscles, preventing her from fleeing (as if there were some other place she'd rather be right now).

He towered over her, never uttering a word, just looking at her with those piercing, bright green eyes. His gaze held promises of unabated pleasure and she had no doubt he could make good on them.

Reaching toward her waist, Ty gently tugged on the end of the satin sash until the garment unraveled, giving him a narrow glimpse of skin vertically along her torso.

Kendall took in a sudden breath as the robe parted. Was this really happening?—

"This thing's been driving me crazy all night",

he confessed hoarsely as the silky belt slid through his fingers.

"Ty, I... we shouldn't..." As if sensing her anxious hesitation, he ran the backs of his knuckles against her cheek reassuringly. "I'm not having sex with you!" she blurted in a nervous rant.

A wicked grin spread across his mouth. "My, my, Kendall—there goes that dirty little mind of yours again."

"I have a dirty mind?" she asked incredulously. "You're the one that untied my robe!"

"Guilty", he confessed. "Never said I was an angel." His mouth pressed against the pulse point on her neck, the rapid flutter of her heartbeat tickling his lips. He nudged the satin garment open as he trailed kisses down her throat and along her collarbone.

Sweet Jesus, she was stunning. No bra—her dark pink nipples already raised, practically begging for his attention. His eyes followed down her soft, feminine torso, finally landing on a pair of barely there, black lace panties.

Kendall could feel his eyes glide down her body, his fiery gaze practically branding her skin. For the most part, she'd always been confident about her body, thankful for the fast metabolism she'd inherited from her mother. It allowed her to eat pretty much anything she wanted without the worry of packing on extra pounds. But something about this moment was different.

Yes, she was tall and skinny, but she didn't look anything like Cameron.

Kendall was small-chested—a B-cup (on a good day). What if he was disappointed in what he saw? Suddenly, her well-known confidence faltered. She attempted to cover herself, but Ty stopped her.

"I want to see you", he insisted.

"I... I'm sorry. I know this is probably not what you're used to—"

"What're you talking about?"

Okay, really? Did she have to spell it out for him? "I don't have... I'm not..." Kendall cupped her hands several inches in front of her breasts as though she were cupping two heavy double Ds.

"Kendall, you're beautiful", he assured her. "So fucking beautiful..." His thumb lightly grazed her pebbled nipple, only to be replaced by his mouth several moments later.

Gasping, Kendall arched her body toward him, running her fingers through his thick blond hair as he suckled her. Her hands held him in place, hopefully conveying to Ty that she was thoroughly enjoying his mouth on her. With every delicate flutter of his tongue, she relaxed, allowing her confidence to rebuild.

His teeth raked against the hard nub as he withdrew and then his mouth migrated to the other side. Her skin was perfumed with a hint of orange blossoms: a scent he was beginning to associate with Kendall.

She always smelled like orange blossoms.

Unbelievable. He'd yet to touch her below the waist and she was already dangerously close to the edge. Had it really been that long since she'd been touched so intimately?—her skin devoured in fiery open-mouth kisses?

Yes.

Too. Damn. Long.

He nipped her lightly with his teeth, and then laved the bite with his tongue, causing goosebumps to spread across the surface of her skin. "Wow", she uttered breathlessly.

"Ditto." His kisses ascended up her chest to her collarbone while his hands wandered up her smooth thighs.

"Ty?"

"Uh-huh..."

His hands were getting close—so close—to where she needed them most. And then one of his thumbs brushed against the sensitive bundle of nerves between her legs, stifling a small gasp. "Never mind. Forgot what I was going to say."

Ty chuckled softly against her neck. "Atta girl. Don't think—just enjoy", he commanded hoarsely. His fingers swept her panties to the side, finding her wet, slick. Ready. He stroked her with the pad of his thumb, provoking a satisfied whimper.

Everything was happening so fast, her body tensing for the impending, glorious release. And then she felt his finger nudge into her... Her hands gripped the front of his shirt as though it were her only lifeline, afraid if she loosened her grasp, she'd levitate in a hypnotic sexual trance.

Damn it. He couldn't believe how hot she was. She was so responsive to his touch. He'd give anything to drive into her. Fast. Hard. Over and over, all night long, until their bodies were completely sated and spent.

But not tonight.

Nope, tonight was all about Kendall. Tonight he'd take pleasure in watching her come. And she was oh-so close. He could feel her body draw tight around his fingers. "Let go, Kendall. I wanna watch you lose control—"

The words had barely left his mouth when the first wave rippled through her, followed by an army of others, each more intense than the one before. Her grip tightened on his shirt as the pleasure pulled her under, enveloping her body with endorphins no drugs on the planet could simulate. Her mouth opened as the cadence continued, completely unaware that she was whispering his name until the surge subsided.

Holy fuck—he'd never been so turned on in his entire life! Her body clamped around his finger like a vice, milking him, drawing him deeper. Those irresistible lips parted slightly in a silent scream—then she'd chanted his name just above a whisper, over and over again. Watching her come with his name on her lips had drained what little blood he'd had left in his brain and sent it surging south to the part of his body throbbing against the fly of his jeans.

Unable to stop himself, he leaned forward and kissed the lips that'd just recited his name like a soulful prayer. Their tongues waltzed in unison. Slipping. Sliding. Gliding effortlessly—comfortably— as though they'd been kissing one another for years.

When he finally pulled back to look at her, her eyes were still closed, her hands still tightly clenched around the front of his shirt. Clearly he'd knocked her off balance. "You okay?"

Nodding, she slowly released his shirt, but couldn't bring herself to look at him yet. Had she really just climaxed in forty-five seconds flat? Her vibrator couldn't even do that!—but Ty's talented fingers certainly had. He'd managed to untie the robe, open her legs and pleasure her—*really pleasure her*— and now he was likely staring, her dewy essence still lingering on his fingers.

"Are you going to look at me?" he whispered.

Kendall shook her head. "Not sure if I can yet."

"Why not?"

Suddenly feeling overexposed (probably because she was the only one with practically no clothes on), she gathered the edges of her robe and wrapped them around her body. Her eyes opened as she tied the sash, although she still managed to avoid eye contact with the man towering over her. Kendall studied her lap as if the right words would suddenly appear there. "I... I didn't mean for things to get this far. God—what you must think about me—"

Ty lifted her chin with his knuckles, forcing her to look into his eyes. "I think you're amazing, Kendall..."

"Well, *obviously*, I think you're amazing, too—"

"Why do I get the feeling there's a *but?*—"

"—*but*, you and me?—*us*...? I just think starting something between us isn't a good idea right now."

His mouth pressed against her lips, nipping, teasing, until her hands cupped his face, holding him steady. He loved how easily she lost control; how easily she forgot her *we're-not-a-good-idea-together* speech. He allowed Kendall to govern the kiss at first, and then he relinquished control again.

Ty wanted to prove a point: they were so good for each other. He needed to chase away her lingering doubts. He broke the kiss suddenly, satisfied with the way she chased his mouth several inches. "You think too much. One day at a time, Doll. One day at a time..."

Chapter 6

"So the police still don't have any leads?" Olivia asked as she joined the group of women already seated at the large patio table. It was a once a month tradition: on the third or fourth Friday of the month, the guys at the fire station would gather at Ty's house for a poker tournament. And their spouses—or girlfriends, in some cases—would congregate on the back patio to chat until the card game was through.

"No", Kendall replied. "Obviously, the creeps knew what they were doing, wearing gloves and masks. I was told by the detectives there was no evidence left behind."

"This is all so weird", Jenny chimed in. "I mean, first the whole arson thing a few months ago, and now this!"

"I know!" Lana agreed. "How on earth did Butler Island suddenly become *crime central?*"

Kendall took a sip of the margarita Lana had prepared for her. "Well, one thing's for sure: things haven't been boring around here!"

"No, they certainly haven't", Olivia admitted.

Life on the island had been pretty interesting, and not just with the sudden spike in crime. Gossip was circulating at mach speeds. Everyone already knew that Ty had been at the pharmacy during the robbery—that was old news. The latest round of juicy gossip had to do with Ty's mammoth-sized white Ford, spotted twice the past week parked in Kendall's driveway. "Okay, I'm just gonna come right out and ask. What's been goin' on between you and Ty?"

Uh-oh. Change the subject—*fast!* "Mmmm", Kendall uttered after swallowing a mouthful of her drink. "This margarita is delicious!—did you make this from scratch?"

"Thanks. Yes, I did—and stop trying to avoid the question", Lana warned. "Inquiring minds want to know…"

Sighing, Kendall conceded. What use was there in denying it? "Okay, I guess there's no point in trying to hide it. We're… well, we're…"

"Playing *hide the salami?*" Jenny asked.

"No! We're… oh, hell—I'm not really sure what it is we're doing, to be honest. I guess you could say we're just taking things one day at a time."

"Honey, I don't want to disappoint you, but that's guy code for 'I want your body—*your naked body*—no-strings-attached!' "

A few of the ladies around the table verbally agreed with Jenny, while others simply nodded. Was that what this thing with Ty was really all about? Was he just using her body?

No, that couldn't be it. Three nights ago, she'd experienced the best orgasm of her life and never once had he hinted she return the favor. If this was purely physical, revolving only around the need for him to find release, wouldn't he have suggested she reciprocate?

"Oh, c'mon, ladies! He just ended his marriage and he's doin' what everyone on the damn island has been houndin' him to do for months: start over", Olivia punctuated. "He's takin' things slow—there's nothing wrong with that." Turning to Kendall, she grabbed her hand and gave it a squeeze. "Ty's a good guy—you know that, right?"

Kendall nodded. "I do."

"Then give him a chance."

Randall Burns stared at his cards, arguments about who'd win next weekend's Super Bowl sputtering around him. Normally he'd be contributing to the chaos, but not tonight. He'd heard the rumors that Ty and Kendall were... *together*. Honestly, he hadn't believed the gossip was entirely accurate. They'd both been at the pharmacy during the robbery and the traumatic experience likely caused a bond to form. *But together...?* He just couldn't see it.

Or maybe he just didn't want to see it.

He and Kendall had a past. They'd been friends—best friends—since middle school. Stayed in contact after she moved away to college and had gladly offered his shoulder for her to cry on when she'd returned to Butler Island after her father's devastating stroke. He wasn't really sure when it'd happened, but somewhere along the way he'd fallen for her.

Early last summer they'd been at the saloon playing a few rounds of pool. The evening was sticky, hot, and the beer was cold and smooth. Conversation was littered with sexual innuendos—not uncommon for the two of them. There was this *aura* between

them that night, a connection so strong—so lustful—
it nearly suffocated him.

After paying their tab that evening he'd driven
her home and had finally given in to temptation.
They'd had hot, wild sex—three times, if he
remembered correctly.

And he remembered every blessed detail.

He'd been on cloud nine until the following
morning when she awoke. Kendall had apologized
repeatedly. He'd tried to explain that he was glad
it'd happened—that he loved her—but she'd called
their wild night a *mistake*... Kendall hadn't dated
anyone since—neither had he.

Randall had been banking on those rumors of
Ty and Kendall *together* being just that: rumors. But
her presence here tonight solidified what he'd feared.

Kendall was moving on.

Unable to suppress the questions lingering on
his tongue any longer, Randall set out to find the
truth. "Noticed you and Kendall have been spending
a lot of time together lately."

Ty tossed several poker chips toward the middle
of the table. "Yeah, so?"

"I think what Burns is trying to say is *back off*",
Grant translated.

"Yeah? Well, we're both adults; I'm single and
so is she. So what's the problem, Rand?"

Releasing a sigh, Randall put his cards face down
on the table. "She's one of my best friends. I care about
her. A lot. And the last thing I want is for her to get
her hopes up, thinking there might actually be something between the two of you, when your only intention is to fuck her."

Ty put his cards down too, his eyes boring holes
into Randall's angry gaze. He knew the guy had a

thing for Kendall, although he hadn't been sure how much so until just now. He liked the guy: he was a hell of a firefighter, and he'd always been one hell of a friend to Olivia growing up. But it was clear they were both interested in the same woman. "What I do—who I decide to do it with—is none of your fucking business, Bro—"

"Hey, hey!" Jimmy Phillips interjected. "C'mon, guys—knock it off!"

For the first time since they began their once a month poker tournament three years ago, the room was eerily quiet.

Running his fingers through his black hair, Randall's attention fell upon Ty again. "Just... don't jerk her around, alright? I don't wanna see her get hurt."

Ty picked up his beer and took an extra-long pull, hoping the ice cold beverage would simmer his growing temper. "Well, then, that makes two of us."

With the tournament now over, the guys spilled onto the patio. Ty couldn't help but think about his earlier discussion with Randall.

Had he missed something?—had there been something serious between Kendall and Rand?

Of course they were best friends. But the way the guy had become infuriated with him made Ty think there was more to it. He made a mental note to ask Kendall about it later, once they were alone.

Until then, he mingled, making sure to keep her in his peripheral. It didn't take long for Randall to make his way over to her. Ty watched discreetly as Rand nestled his lips against her ear, whispering something that made Kendall smile. Moments later the two walked toward the opposite side of the pool, engaging in a private conversation.

Chatter seemed to fade into the background as Ty's focus settled on them. What he wouldn't give for the ability to read lips.

Placing his hands on the back of Kendall's chair, Randall leaned forward until his lips were but an inch away from her ear. "Bet your head's about to explode. You ready to be rescued from Gossipville, Babe?"

Kendall couldn't help but smile. Rand knew she wasn't fond of the island's favorite pastime. "Calgon, take me away." She followed Rand to the opposite side of the patio, unable to ignore the force with which his jaw clenched. "You saved me just in time", she joked as they came to a halt. "I think my brain's turning to mush!"

"You know I always look out for you."

"Yeah, I know", she admitted softly.

Randall sighed, staring at the ground. "I, uh, wasn't expecting to see you here tonight... You and Everitt, huh?"

"It's nothing serious, Rand. We're just..."

"Just what?"

Wrapping her arms around her middle for warmth, as well as comfort, she replied, "We're just taking things a day at a time. Exploring our feelings for one another."

"And you think he's ready for that? You honestly think he wants anything to do with a commitment right now?"

Kendall tucked a strand of hair behind her ear.

This wasn't easy: she knew Randall still had feelings for her. But it'd been well over seven months since they'd slept together. It'd been a mistake, through and through. Making a spontaneous decision to have sex with your best friend tended to muddy the water. Randall wanted to make something of it; she just wanted things to revert back to how it'd always been between them.

It wasn't that she didn't want to feel more for him. Randall knew her—really knew her—inside and out. Knew her dreams, her secrets, her flaws and loved her anyway. He was gorgeous: stood just over six feet with thick black hair, had eyes the color of stainless steel, and a body one would expect from a professional athlete.

He was the epitome of the perfect man, yet she didn't get that jittery sensation in the pit of her gut like she did when she looked at Ty. "Does it really matter? I'm not after anything serious."

Randall gave her *the look*: the one where his right brow arched and his steel gray eyes transformed into intense laser beams. His "bullshit detector" as he often called it, because one glance at his expression typically caused all *bullshit* to cease. It was like a damn truth serum or something. In fact, she'd told him numerous times to find a way to bottle and sell it to police agencies across the country; even the hardest of criminals would succumb to that look!

"Okay. So I wouldn't exactly be opposed to something serious, but—"

"You're gonna get hurt, Ken."

"I'm not naïve, you know? He's newly divorced; I get it. Settling down again is probably the furthest thing from his mind right now—"

"Damn straight, it is. The only thing a guy in his position is thinking about is where his next piece of ass will come from."

"Okay, now you're just being ridiculous. We're—"

"Have you slept with him?"

"No!"

"But you're plannin' on it, aren't you?"

This was turning ugly—fast. She tried to remind herself that his line of questioning was coming from a good place. He loved her, and watching her pursue a relationship with another man was most likely shredding his insides to pieces. "That's none of your business, Rand", she uttered through clenched teeth.

He studied her: shoulders set, chin lifted, arms crossed. Yep, she was pissed. He'd taken it too far—miles past concern—and had let his jealousy get the better of him. He needed to regain his self-control. Because if he didn't, he'd end up pushing Kendall directly into Ty's arms—and that was the last thing he wanted. What he needed to do was back off and just be there for her. Because when Everitt shattered her heart into a million little pieces—and no doubt, he would—Randall would be there to mend it back together again.

Reaching for her, he pulled her against his chest and savored the sensation of her body against his. "I'm sorry. It's just... I don't want to see you get hurt. I love you, you know that?"

Kendall rested her forehead against his chest. "I know", she whispered.

"Guess this day was bound to come, huh?"

"Yeah." It pained her to see him this way. She didn't want to hurt him.

"Guess we better get back over there before we cause a scene", Randall suggested, and then kissed the top of her head.

They turned back toward the patio to rejoin the group. All eyes were on them (so much for not making a scene). Ty's gaze fell upon her, questions swimming in their depths.

Good. Because she had some questions of her own.

Chapter 7

Couples slowly started pairing off and soon it was just Kendall and Ty that remained. They sat next to one another on the brown wicker loveseat, Jimmy Buffet's *Son of a Sailor* filling the silence lurking between them.

"So what'd you think about your first poker night?" Ty finally asked as he placed his hand on her knee.

"It was fun."

"Yeah?"

Kendall smiled. "Yeah."

"This sort of thing doesn't usually happen, you know?"

"What are you talking about?" she questioned confusedly.

"Drama. Well, at least not with the guys, anyway..."

Kendall closed her eyes for a moment and drew a deep breath. "Please tell me Rand didn't start anything with you."

Shrugging his shoulders a bit, Ty turned his

attention toward her. "We had a few words—it was nothing. Kind of got me thinking, though."

"About what?"

He paused for a moment, organizing the many questions lingering on the tip of his tongue. Not wanting to come across as though he were interrogating her, he decided to ask the one that mattered most. "How do you feel about Randall?—because if there's something going on between the two of you, I don't want to get in the middle of it."

"He's my best friend—"

"And he's obviously in love with you."

Kendall nodded her head in agreement. "Yes, he is. But the feeling isn't mutual... I love him, too—but only as a friend. Nothing more."

Ty unveiled a sexy grin and then brushed his thumb against her bottom lip. "I was hoping you'd say that."

For several moments, neither of them uttered a word. Their eyes met, searched, and assessed what the other was thinking, feeling.

Licking her suddenly dry lips, Kendall cut in on their unspoken exchange. "It's getting late. I have an early start tomorrow. Guess we'd better call it a night."

His fingertips trailed down the outside of her arm, his eyes following their path until he spoke. "Guess we'd better get you to bed then, huh?"

His expression left nothing to the imagination, his intentions blatantly clear: he wasn't tucking her into bed—he was *taking* her to bed...

Oh boy...

It was after ten o'clock, but the night was still

young. Kendall sat in the passenger seat in Ty's truck, her heart thrashing about in her chest. They hadn't spoken since they'd left the patio moments earlier, and for that she was thankful. Because she wasn't entirely confident she'd be able to form a single, coherent sentence. She stole a quick glance at Ty from the corner of her eye. He was casually leaned back in his seat, one hand on the wheel, the other lazily stroking the short stubble along his angular jaw. Confidence seemed to roll off him in waves. And that was causing her hands to shake in anticipation.

Because there was nothing sexier than a man who was comfortable and confident in his own skin. Especially when said skin was rippled with hard muscle underneath.

The ride seemed like an eternity, but likely only took three or four minutes. By the time he man-euvered his truck into her driveway, the sexual tension was like a third passenger wedged between them: a living, breathing entity.

The key had barely left the ignition before Ty vacated the driver's seat, reappearing moments later at her door. He gave the handle a firm tug and then offered his hand. Kendall got the feeling the action was more than a chivalrous gesture. Taking his hand held a hidden meaning: acceptance. He wanted to pick up where they'd left off the other night and accepting his hand was a nonverbal confirmation that she wanted that, too.

Kendall placed her hand in his, allowing Ty to assist her to the ground. Once her feet were planted firmly on the pavement, he intertwined their fingers, leading her up the stone walkway, up the front porch steps, until they reached the front door. Kneeling, she lifted the doormat with her free hand in search of the spare key. She'd barely managed to get back to her feet before Ty's mouth settled over hers.

He couldn't recall the last time he'd wanted something—someone—so much. Unable to control the desire to touch her, taste her, he reached behind her head and devoured her luscious mouth with his kiss. He could still taste the remnants of lime, tequila and salt from the margarita she'd had earlier, and savored the flavor of raw lust on his tongue. Never had he tasted a combination so delicious, so sweet.

One hand still cupping the back of her head, his other disentangled from her grip and begin wandering down her side, along her hip, then behind. He gripped her backside through her jeans, kneading his fingers into her firm flesh, and then pulled her even closer so that nothing but the thin denim fabric stood between them.

The heat from his body penetrated her clothes, sizzling her skin. Was this really happening?

She was making out with Ty Everitt on her front porch...

Clearly she'd inhaled too much testosterone during the ride home (probably should have cracked the window open a bit).

One of her hands rested against his chest, the cadence of his rapid heartbeat tapping against her palm; the other hand lay on his shoulder, fingers still holding the key with an easy grip. The swell of his sex pressed against her as their hips collided. She heard a low groan escape from the back of his throat, and the next thing she knew, he was wrestling the key from her fingertips.

Ty managed to unlock the door, turn the knob,

and open it without separating their mouths. He backed her inside and then kicked the door shut with his foot. More than anything, he wanted to take her up against the door. Right here. Right now. Wanted to drive into her with an animal-like ferocity, hear her scream, begging him not to stop. Make her feel better than she'd ever felt before.

But this woman deserved better than that. Taking her up against the door would come later.

Their mouths continued devouring, nibbling, tasting—only separating long enough to remove each other's shirts before meeting again. Slowly they made their way up the wooden staircase, leaving behind a trail of clothes in their wake. By the time they made it to the loft bedroom, they were both completely topless—Ty's shoes and Kendall's boots had also vanished.

"I want you", Ty graveled against her mouth. He could feel her lips ascend into a smile, reaffirming she felt the same way. And once he had that silent confirmation, his mouth embarked on a journey. He kissed his way down her throat, down her chest, and then detoured toward one of her breasts. He sucked hard and then nipped her dark pink nipple with his teeth before lapping the sensitive nub with his tongue.

"*Oh, yes*", she whispered. Every slick caress of his tongue caused the ache between her legs to heighten.

Not wanting to leave her other breast untouched, he repeated the same routine on the other side.

And then that gifted mouth of his was on the move again. Heading south.

Kneeling in front of her, he trailed soft kisses down her belly, over her navel, until he came upon the top of her jeans. He unfastened the button and lowered the zipper, relishing the sound of Kendall's sudden intake of breath—and the sight of her soft stomach quivering—as he tugged on the waistband.

Ty drew the denim over her hips, down her long lean legs. "Step out of these, Doll", he commanded hoarsely. He felt her hands settle on his shoulders for balance, and then one at a time, she lifted her feet, the sight of her candy apple red polish almost causing him to hyperventilate.

His large callused hands journeyed up the backs of her legs, his fingertips caressing every contour, stroking her skin as though he were a blind man reading Braille. Higher and higher his hands traveled, over the curve of her firm bottom, until one settled on the small of her back, the other delicately tracing the thin segment of lace that stretched across her hip. His fingertips snagged the dainty, white lace, and then finally settled on the miniature red bow attached to the top, just above her mound. Red ribbon: the kind you'd expect to find at the finish line of a world-renowned race.

And the grand prize was the ravishing, Kendall Porter.

"Pretty", he uttered as his index finger lightly tapped the bow.

The sensation of his hands on her body was almost more than she could take. He touched her with confidence, his skilled hands having mastered the intricacies of the female body.

Rising from his knees, he stood, slowly backing her further into the loft, until the backs of her knees collided against the bed. Kendall sat along the edge and gave his body the careful attention she'd just received. Her fingertips trailed down the hard plane of his chest, down the rippled contours of his six-pack abs, down the narrow path of dark hair that disappeared behind the fly of his jeans.

She wasn't sure what turned her on more: the look and feel of his conditioned body, or the fact that he was taking great pleasure in watching her as she explored every mouthwatering inch.

Just as he did moments earlier, she released the button to his jeans, lowered the zipper, and then tucked her fingertips underneath the waistband of his boxer briefs before tugging them down a bit.

She sat there in awe for a few moments just looking at him, unable to make a sound. Her eyes widened as she assessed his size (guess the old saying about a man with large feet really *was* true after all).

Because "big" was an understatement.

Reaching forward, she gripped his hard length and stroked him firmly—slowly—until a bead of thick fluid appeared on the bulbous tip. Inching closer, she lapped the liquid with her tongue, savoring the flavor of Ty's salty essence, relishing the low groan that escaped his lips. His fingers tangled in her hair as she took him into her mouth.

Sweet baby Jesus... The sensation of Kendall's hot, wet mouth—the image of those perfectly voluptuous lips clamped around his cock—would be forever etched in his mind.

He was watching her, his eyes intensely focused on her as inch by inch, his rigid length disappeared into her mouth. His fingers tugged gently around her hair, his hips rocked forward ever so slightly as she devoured him, his low groans—almost animal-like—assuring her he was quickly losing control.

And it was that sudden realization that made the delightful tingle between her legs transform into an overwhelming throb.

Afraid he'd burst if her mouth continued its assault on his cock any longer, he cupped her face and met her amber, wanton gaze. "If you don't stop, this'll be over before we even begin, Doll." That luscious mouth of hers curved upward in a sexy grin. And that nearly did him in.

Kendall leaned back on her hands, scooting her bottom back toward the silver metal headboard. Lying back on her elbows, she observed as Ty rolled a condom down his engorged length, and then stepped out of his dark denim jeans.

And then like a predator stalking its prey, he crawled toward her on his hands and knees, until his sculpted body hovered over hers.

He bathed her body in open-mouth kisses while his hands migrating down the sides of her lean silhouette. The next thing she knew, he'd hooked his fingers under the waistband of her panties and had miraculously tossed them aside, leaving her completely bare.

His eyes perused her naked body, silently savoring every flawless inch.

Normally Kendall wasn't a prude: she'd bared all in front of a man before. But as his eyes slowly raked along the surface of her skin, she suddenly felt shy, uneasy. He concentrated as though he was studying a map, intensely focused on memorizing the routes to every erogenous zone on her body.

Self-conscious under his careful scrutiny, she moved her arms to cover herself.

"Don't", he pleaded gruffly as he grabbed her wrists. "You're gorgeous." Ty pinned her arms above her head while his mouth came down over one of her breasts, suckling gently until her body wriggled beneath him.

Tension was building low in her belly, causing the ache between her legs to become almost unbearable.

Sensing her need to be touched, Ty repositioned her wrists, holding them in place with his left hand, while his right journeyed south between her legs.

The moment she felt his fingers on her throbbing center, her hips bucked. He strummed her as though she were an acoustic guitar, performing a soothing ballad—except the melodies were emanating from her lips instead of a musical instrument.

Holy fuck... Ty watched in awe. Kendall Porter was a living, breathing fantasy.

"Ty, please", she whimpered.

"Tell me... Tell me what you want", he urged.

The things he was doing to her—the way he was making her feel—made her forget about her earlier insecurities. She knew what she wanted. And suddenly she wasn't afraid to ask for it. "Make me come..."

Ty's mouth turned upward in a sexy grin. "Yes ma'am..."

His fingers slid into her tight heat as his thumb worked over the small bundle of nerve endings in soft, lazy circles. He stifled a groan as she dug her heels into the mattress, lifting her bottom to meet his thrusting fingers. And then he felt the first contraction pulse around his fingers.

God, she was so beautiful. Her normal olive skin tone seemed to blush; ink black hair framed her pretty face, spilling onto the pale blue comforter like black sun rays; lush lips parted in a silent scream as pleasure pummeled through her. Flawless.

Mesmerizing.

Unable to curb his desire any longer, Ty plunged into her primed body, burying himself to the hilt.

Kendall gasped as her body stretched to accommodate his colossal dimensions, feeling as though her core was completely pervaded.

"Oh, yeah... Kendall...*fuck*, you feel so good..."

Arms still pinned above her head, she managed to wrestle them free, eager to begin roaming over his hard body. The muscles in his arms bulged as he hovered above her; his chest was solid, strong; his stomach was patterned with ridges and valleys.

Ty was perfection...

The thrust and retreat may have started slow, but the pace quickly hastened. Pent-up lust caused the gentle, savory sex to turn wild, fiery. Dirty.

Their bodies collided. Hard. Fast.

Kendall could feel the tension building again, drawing tight.

Thrust. Retreat. Thrust. Retreat.

"Please! Don't stop!"

Thrust. Retreat. Thrust. Retreat.

Nails raked across his back, hurting *so good.*

Thrust. Retreat.

Harder. Faster.

The pressure was more than Kendall could bear. And like a dam bursting, her body flooded with a surge of dashing heat.

Rushing through her veins. Zipping down her spine, stimulating every nerve ending.

"Oh, God... Ty..."

Her body was gripping him, drawing him deeper. He could feel his balls draw up and then...

He was free-falling over the edge, Kendall's beautiful body cushioning the impending blow. His body was enveloped in ecstasy, hardly feeling her teeth nip into his shoulder as they relinquished control together.

Ty's large frame collapsed over her trembling body while he caught his breath. He lay there for several moments, trying to collect his thoughts, and then finally rose. "Be right back", he assured her as he casually strolled toward the bathroom.

Kendall rolled over and reached for the teal robe draped over the antique slipper chair wedged in the corner. Quickly she covered her body and began tying the sash when Ty emerged from the bathroom.

The moment he clapped eyes on her, he sensed her uneasiness. Kendall was avoiding eye contact, intensely focused on her hands as they worked to anchor her robe. He took the opportunity to put his boxer briefs back on and then slid into his jeans. Once they were fastened, he ambled toward her.

"I'm sorry. I—"

Ty interrupted Kendall's apology with a lazy, gentle kiss. "Well, I'm not..."

Gnawing on her bottom lip, she finally smiled. "Look, I don't normally do this sort of thing."

"Me either..."

Kendall hugged herself, suddenly needing comfort. More than anything, she wanted to ask him what this meant. Wanted him to clarify exactly where they stood, but instead remained quiet. She was afraid of hearing the truth: to him, it meant nothing...

"Guess I should go."

"Um, yeah. I have to get up early and—" Ty turned his back and headed down the stairs. Kendall followed cautiously, eyeing him as he collected the rest of his clothes scattered along the steps. By the time they'd reached the front door, the silence was encroaching into awkwardness.

"I had fun tonight, Doll", Ty stated casually.

Kendall tucked a strand of hair behind her ear and smiled shyly. "Me, too."

After kissing her cheek, he turned toward the door. "I'll call you."

"Um, okay..."

She stood there in a trance, staring at the heavy front door for some time, the outspoken inner voice repeatedly chanting an alarming message:

You took the bait—hook, line, and sinker. Be prepared to be thrown back...

Chapter 8

Kendall and Vicki meandered through the Mainland Mall, just outside of Apalachicola for a fun-filled day of girl talk and shopping. Kendall had promised to accompany her after discovering Vicki's visible panty lines at the annual New Year's Eve Bonfire, but had been unable to manage a full day off from the pharmacy until now.

They'd already enjoyed a light lunch in the food court and had arrived at Victoria's Secret in search of new, feminine undergarments to replace Vicki's plain, outdated collection. They stood in front of a large round table covered in lace and cotton thongs in every color and pattern imaginable. The sale sign indicated the panties were *buy four, get the fifth free*, leaving Vicki to sift through the vast assortment to find the styles she preferred.

It'd been nearly two weeks since Kendall's—ahem—*fun with Ty*. After he left that evening, she'd collapsed onto her bed and had relived every tantalizing detail. She'd awoke the following morning, her girl parts deliciously sore, wearing a dreamy grin that screamed, *"I just got laid!"* She'd expected to hear from him at some point that day... only she hadn't.

In fact, she hadn't spoken to Ty since he'd left that evening.

Nearly two weeks ago...

The silence was telling, really. She didn't need some lame excuse; Ty's actions spoke volumes.

He wasn't interested in *her*—just having *sex* with her.

Damn it, she was such a fool.

As a matter of fact, Ty was probably having a good belly laugh at her expense.

She should have seen this coming. It wasn't as if she hadn't been warned. Lana and Jenny both cautioned her at poker night (and let's not forget about her little spat with Randall).

"You okay?" Vicki questioned. "You've been staring into space for the last five minutes."

"I'm sorry, Vic. There's a lot going on at the pharmacy with this new security system I had installed a few days ago", she lied. No one knew about her erotic evening with Ty—not even Olivia. She didn't want to be dishonest. She just wanted to forget it'd happened. "I promise to give you my undivided attention for the remainder of the day."

"Good—'cause I really need your help! Valentine's day is in two days", she gestured with her fingers, "and I want to find something really sexy to wear for Alex."

"Okay", Kendall murmured excitedly as she rubbed her palms together. "What do you normally wear to bed?"

Vicki shrugged. "Usually one of Alex's T-shirts and a pair of fuzzy socks."

Kendall's shoulders slumped in disappointment. "*Fuzzy socks?*"

"My feet get cold at night!" she countered.

"So tell Alex to crank the thermostat up a bit! Fuzzy socks—really?" Blushing, Vicki nodded. "Well", Kendall began on a sigh, "guess I have my work cut out for me."

They browsed the racks for a bit, searching for the perfect piece for a lingerie beginner. They finally stumbled upon a display at the front of the store with garments less daring than they'd seen already. Kendall reached for a sheer ensemble hanging on the wall. "Something like this is perfect to start off with if you're not used to wearing lingerie. They call this a babydoll. It still covers all the essential parts, but the sheer fabric will allow Alex to see that incredible figure of yours."

Vicki eyed the delicate-looking garment carefully. "You sure about this?"

"Of course, I'm sure! And it's festive." Kendall shook the hanger excitedly. "Comes in red…" This was a huge step for her friend. The girl had never worn a thong in her life and she was but moments away from purchasing her very first negligee. Sensing Vicki's apprehension, Kendall set out to reassure her. "Trust me, honey—Alex will drool when he sees you in this."

"You think so?"

Kendall nodded.

"Okay, I guess I'll go try it on." Vicki took the babydoll and strolled toward the back of the store. "Be back in a few minutes", she called over her shoulder.

Browsing while she waited for Vic, she approached the opposite wall that displayed the more *risqué* collection. Kendall lifted a pink push-up bustier and matching thong from the rack, holding it out in front of her for closer inspection. The shade reminded her of cotton candy, which was likely why it was available in this particular hue: in a man's eye, a woman wearing this would most certainly appear edible.

"I'd pay good money to see you in that..."

There was no need to turn around; she'd recognize that voice anywhere.

Ty.

She returned the bustier to the rack. "Well, I guess it's a good thing I'm not for sale, then." Kendall kept her eyes on the selection along the wall, slowly ambling toward the back of the store, unable to completely ignore the handsome man subtly following behind.

"How've you been?" he finally asked.

"Never better..."

"Good", he commented as he nodded. "What brings you here?"

"Just shopping..."

"You plan on buying anything in this store?"

"Wouldn't you like to know", she whispered over her shoulder.

His pace still one step behind hers, he replied, "Yeah, I would, actually. Can't help but wonder about the lucky guy that gets to see you in this stuff." That certainly got her attention. She pivoted in a flash, her eyes beaming with anger and regret.

"That's none of your business, Ty."

"You're mad at me", he acknowledged flatly.

"No, not at you— at *myself.*"

Alright, Everitt, it's time to do some serious apologizing. "Listen, I know I—"

Kendall put her palm up in front of her. "Save

it. I'm not getting into this with you right now."

Shifting his weight a bit, he shoved his hands in his pockets. "Okay, when?"

Just then, Vicki came strolling out of the dressing room. "Think I'm gonna take this—*Oh—hey, Ty.*"

"Hey, Vic", he greeted, his eyes never swaying from Kendall.

Vicki's head snapped from side-to-side like a spectator's at a tennis match, observing the non-verbal argument unfolding between her friends. "Okaaay, I think I'm just gonna go pay for this", she uttered before turning toward the registers.

"*When?*" Ty insisted again.

"I'm busy today—busy with a friend who took the time to *call me.*"

Kendall turned away and left him standing in the middle of Victoria's Secret like the damn idiot he was.

Yeah, he wasn't proud of his disappearing act. It was juvenile—no doubt about it. He needed to make things right and he knew just where to start. He waited for Kendall and Vicki to exit the store and then set his sights on the pale pink ensemble he'd seen her looking at when he'd first spotted her.

"Excuse me, sir. Can I help you?" the young attendant asked.

"Hope so. The gorgeous dark-haired woman that was just at the register... What size would she wear in this?" he asked as he gestured toward the wall display.

The attendant smiled and then plucked a small from the rack. "Is this gift a surprise?"

Ty chuckled under his breath and then read her name tag. "Mandy, you have no idea..."

* * * * *

The following evening, Ty sat across from Chief
Handler at the fire station, scanning over a report
one of the guys had written after responding to a call
earlier in the day.

Typically he spent the night shift at the station
alone.

Roughly eighteen months ago, the city experienced a budget crisis, threatening to eliminate four
firefighter positions and three at B.I.P.D. After racking
their brains for weeks, they'd finally reached a
solution: revert to twelve-hour shifts, instead of the
usual twenty-four. The city issued on-call phones to
every firefighter in the department in the event an
emergency occurred during the evening hours (all
but the three lieutenants who were still required to
work the full twenty-four). After all, *somebody* had to
drive the engine to the determined destination.

The guys had all left about twenty minutes ago,
leaving him to wonder why Chief was still loitering
around. "I have this under control, Chief. Why don't
you call it a night and head home?"

"Can't yet."

Ty tore his attention away from the report,
giving the large man who'd been the closest thing to
a father since his parents passed, a thorough analysis.
"Uh-oh, I know that look. Your heartburn acting up
again?"

"Is it really that obvious?" Chief Handler asked
as he patted his large belly.

Nodding, Ty gestured toward the two empty
takeout containers still visible on the edge of the
table. "Yeah. And I put two and two together."

"Debbie made meatloaf tonight. I hate it when
she makes that junk! Doesn't have a lick of flavor

and it's the consistency of a damn hockey puck!"

"If she knows you don't like it, why go through the trouble to make it?"

"Well, probably because she doesn't exactly know how terrible I think it is", Chief explained as he winced.

"Ah... The old *'feed it to the dog when the wife isn't looking'* act, huh?"

"I tried, but even the damn dog doesn't want anything to do with it! So now, I hang out here on meatloaf nights, scarf down takeout from the diner, and when I get home, I tell her I ate a salad at the station."

Ty laughed. "A salad?—and she believes you?"

Chief massaged the heel of his hand firmly against his breastbone. "Normally she does, but no way can I go home with this heartburn—she'll know immediately I didn't eat a salad."

Ty eyed the empty containers again. "What *did* you eat?"

"Two double bacon cheeseburgers, a double order of fries, coleslaw, a pickle spear—"

"And a partridge in a pear tree", Ty added wryly. "No wonder you have heartburn!"

"I know—probably should've stuck to a single order of fries, and I would have if I'd realized I was out of Tums."

Hmmm. No Tums.

He'll have to buy more at the pharmacy. Kendall's pharmacy...

"No worries, Chief. I'll take the rescue truck and head to the pharmacy before it closes. You wouldn't want anyone in town to see you buying antacids—that'd get back to Debbie before you'd make it home..."

Chapter 9

Ty maneuvered the rescue truck into the fire lane in front of Porter Pharmacy (just one of the many perks of being a lieutenant at the fire department). A quick scan of the street indicated the store was empty.

Good. Because he wanted Kendall's undivided attention.

He hadn't spoken to her since their run-in at the mall yesterday. She was mad at him—that much was obvious. She hadn't wanted to hash things out in the middle of Victoria's Secret yesterday. Hadn't wanted to make a scene.

Hallelujah. Because there's nothing quite like a lover's quarrel in the middle of a lingerie store (that tended to put a damper on sales rather quickly). Kendall Porter had class and dignity, preferring a more private environment to face-off with him. He admired her for that.

Because his ex-wife would've caused a scene. A big one.

His calls had went unanswered last night—no surprise there. Clearly she was avoiding him. But here at the pharmacy, she couldn't...

Drawing in a hefty liter of air, Ty exhaled slowly and then emerged from the ambulance. After entering the store, he strolled toward the empty pharmacy counter in the back and tapped his palm over the small bell lying in front of the register.

And then he waited...

"Be there in just a sec", Kendall shouted from her office. She placed the last label on the handful of prescriptions she'd just bagged and then rose from her chair. "Twenty more minutes", she mumbled under her breath as she stole a glimpse at the time. Gathering the small paper bags on her desk, she started toward the counter, alphabetizing the prescriptions while on the move.

"Just when I thought you couldn't look any prettier, you come out here wearing those."

Kendall froze mid-step, astonished to find Ty standing on the opposite side of the counter. Suddenly it occurred to her what he was referring to: she was wearing her glasses. Reaching up with her free hand, she adjusted the black plastic frames and then cleared her throat.

"Had some problems with my contacts this morning", she clarified. There was no need to go into detail. Ty didn't need to know she'd barely slept a wink last night, tossing, thinking about him. And when her alarm sounded this morning, she'd been so tired, her contacts had taken an unexpected plunge into the toilet.

"What are you doing here?" she asked directly.

"We really need to work on your customer service—"

"My customer service is just fine—thank you, very much—and you know what I meant."

Ty put his hands up in surrender. "Relax, Doll. Chief Handler sent me here for some Tums."

"Oh." Funny, she couldn't help but feel a little twinge of disappointment. Of course he wasn't here to patch things up with her (not that she wanted him to or anything). "Antacids are midway down aisle two, on your left."

Smiling, he shoved one of his hands in his pockets. "Be right back..."

Her eye's tracked him until he disappeared down aisle two and once he was out of sight, Kendall reached into her bottom drawer for her compact. She quickly applied a dab of powder to her nose and forehead, and then smoothed her hair a bit before placing it back into the well-organized drawer.

She then turned her attention to the prescriptions she'd carried from her office, making sure to place them in the pick-up basket located behind her while she waited.

Damn it, what's taking him so long? "You do know I'm closing in five minutes", she called out over her shoulder.

Silence.

Kendall sighed. *Men... point 'em in the right direction and they'll still manage to get lost.*

Squaring her shoulders, she willed her body to move, pointing her three-inch black heels toward aisle two. Turning the corner, she found Ty casually leaning against the support post in the middle of the aisle.

God, he looked delicious (especially in his uniform). *Stop—you're mad at him, remember?* "Find what you were looking for?" she asked.

Revealing that seductive grin of his, he pushed away from the pole and slowly walked toward her. "Think I just did."

Their eyes met and held for a few long beats. And then as if finally coming to her senses, Kendall looked away. "Let me ring that up for you", she uttered as she turned to leave.

Reaching for her, Ty caught her arm, preventing her hasty escape. "Okay, how long are we gonna ignore this thing between us?"

Yanking her arm out of his grasp, she crossed them in front of her. "Interesting word choice: *ignore*. It's been two weeks since you've bothered to speak to me. Seems if anyone's 'ignoring' this thing between us, it's you!"

Rocking back on his heels, he shoved his free hand back into his pocket. "Alright, I deserve that", he acknowledged, nodding. "Listen, I'm sorry. The last thing I meant to do was hurt you."

She wanted to be mad at him. Wanted to watch him squirm—agonize over upsetting her—but she just couldn't do it. His apology seemed genuine and sincere. "I know", she whispered.

Relieved, Ty smiled. "Any plans tomorrow?"

"I have to work."

"And after?"

Kendall raked her teeth across her bottom lip, deciphering how to answer his inquisition. "I'll be really busy", she finally declared as she turned toward the register."

Ty followed behind, waiting until she settled behind the counter before he inquired further into her plans. "Busy, huh?"

"Uh-huh."

"So... you have a date or something?"

"Sort of", she replied as she began ringing up the bottle of Tums.

Ty laid a ten dollar bill on the counter. "Sort of? Doll, either you have a date or you don't."

The register drawer opened. Kendall placed the ten in its corresponding place and began collecting dollars and coins. She handed Ty his change and then tucked a strand of hair behind her ear. "Does a date with a half gallon of ice cream count?"

Ty released a breath he hadn't been aware he was holding and smiled. He was beginning to think he'd blown his chance with Kendall for good. He'd really missed her. Missed her sarcasm, her distinct laugh. Her body.

But he'd needed time away to figure out what he wanted. And now that he knew...

"You had me worried there for a sec. I was actually beginning to wonder if I had some real competition."

"Oh, you do", she assured him. "I'm a sucker for orange sherbet. It's right up there with onion rings."

"Ouch!" Ty cried as he reached for his chest. "Guess I sort of had that one coming."

Kendall laughed. "That was quite the Academy performance, Lieutenant. I think you might've found your calling."

Tension seemed to vanish as the aura between them reverted back to its normal, playful position. And as the laughter faded, Ty's expression turned serious. "Look, I know I'm probably doing this whole thing ass backwards, but... have dinner with me tomorrow."

"Ty—"

"I promise not to cut-in to too much of your

orange sherbet time."

"Do you know what tomorrow is?" she asked cautiously.

"Tuesday." Ty laughed again when Kendall playfully rolled her eyes. "Okay, it's Valentine's Day", he corrected.

"And you're okay with that?—because you know how it's going to be interpreted. It'll be the juiciest gossip to circulate since the robbery a few weeks ago."

Ty gripped the edge of the counter, amused over her reluctance to be seen in public with him. "Yes, I'm well aware. So?—what do you say?"

That powerful inner voice was speaking to her again: *Fool me once, shame on you. Fool me twice…* Sometimes she wished she could slap a muzzle on that damn voice. This time, she'd be more careful. This time, she wouldn't lose her self-control. "I get off at seven tomorrow."

"I'll be by to pick you up at your place at a quarter till eight."

Chapter 10

Ty finished packing the supplies for his date with Kendall, making sure to hide the evidence behind the driver's seat of his four-door truck.

Backing out of the driveway, he thought about her as he drove. His attempts to keep his distance after they'd slept together had been incredibly difficult. But he'd needed to sort things out in his mind.

He'd made this mistake before: rushing into a relationship with a woman he'd been extremely infatuated with. And he wasn't big on repeating mistakes.

Truthfully, he was scared to death. Because that one night with Kendall had been more amazing than six years of hot sex with his ex-wife.

Yeah. The realization had nearly sucked the air from his lungs.

For two weeks he avoided her, which hadn't been an easy feat—not by a long shot.

He'd been cranky, miserable. Visions of Kendall's naked body writhing beneath him haunted his dreams and lingered in the forefront of his mind while he was awake.

Let's just take things one day at a time. See where this leads, he'd told her. And when fate led the two of them to her bed?

They'd created magic—except he'd ruined it by performing a Houdini act, disappearing like a fucking pussy.

He was man enough to admit it.

And now he was trying to make things right. He wanted to pursue this thing with Kendall—not because it was morally correct—but because it's what he wanted. She was what he wanted.

Turning into her driveway, Ty emerged from his truck, leaving the diesel engine running. Every step brought him closer, each one causing his heart to flutter. By the time he reached the front porch, it was hard to decipher when one beat ended and another began.

Sucking in a deep breath, Ty rang the doorbell and moments later, Kendall appeared in a strapless red jumpsuit, her tiny waist cinched with a braided beige belt. His eyes traveled down the length of her body. "Wow…" A sudden sharp pain resided in his chest, causing him to wonder if he'd been struck by Cupid's arrow.

Kendall glanced down at her clothes, nervously sweeping her hands down the front of her thighs. "Hope this is okay—I wasn't sure how to dress since the only hint you gave me was that we'd be outside."

"You look amazing."

Meeting his gaze, she smiled. "Thank you."

Their eyes held for a short time, the idle of the diesel engine the only sound. "I, uh, guess we should get going", he finally managed as he offered his hand. He chuckled under his breath as she stepped around him, keeping both hands firmly gripped around her small purse as she descended down the porch steps.

Jogging ahead of her, Ty opened the passenger door.

"What is it with you *island boys* and your big trucks?—it's like everyone's trying to overcome-pensate for something", she uttered as she climbed in.

Ty bit back a grin as he closed her door, rushing around the front of his truck to get in on the other side. "That may be true for some, but not all of us", he countered.

Oh boy. That sexy smirk, coupled with a flirty wink, was a deadly combination. She could feel her cheeks flush as she recalled the memory of Ty's naked body...

Okay, so maybe he was the exception to the rule.

Forcing the delicious vision aside, she turned her focus toward the evening's agenda "So where *are* we going, if you don't mind me asking?"

Ty reached for her hand, interlocking their fingers together, relieved when she didn't pull away. "You'll see. Good things come to those who wait..."

Promise? She wanted to ask, but instead re-mained quiet. And then as if remembering what'd happened after the last time she'd sat in this seat, she reached for the controls and cracked her window a bit.

Because clearly, she was beginning to exhibit signs of testosterone poisoning.

And holding her breath wasn't an option.

"You hot?—I can turn on the air."

"Nope—just need a little fresh air." *Or a gas mask.*

The remainder of the ride was driven in relative silence, until the truck rolled to a stop along the abandoned stretch of road on the Northwest tip of the island.

"We're here", Ty announced.

Kendall peered through the windshield, although she couldn't see a darn thing. The Northwest segment of Butler Island was undeveloped, secluded. There were no homes, no businesses, no lights—just a pristine coastline.

Ty snagged the basket wedged behind his seat and then came around to the passenger side. "You gonna sit there all night?"

"What are you up to?" Kendall asked cautiously.

Offering his hand, he smiled. "Come with me and find out."

She eyed his hand for several moments before finally giving in. The moon was but a tiny sliver in the sky, reflecting just enough light for Kendall to see the large silhouette in front of her.

Leaving the truck behind, Ty carefully led her over the small sand dunes to an awaiting pile of wood. "Hang on; this'll only take a sec." Placing the basket in the sand, he knelt in front of the pile. The strike of a match cut through the steady sound of waves lapping against the shore, and within moments the flames flickered to life.

With the beach suddenly aglow, Ty spread the blanket over the sand and gestured for Kendall to take a seat.

"Whatcha got in the basket?" she asked as she tucked her legs underneath her.

"Chinese takeout. Probably not the most romantic Valentine's cuisine, but I figured it was the easiest to eat out here." He unpacked several containers from the basket, placing the cartons between them. "I wasn't sure what you liked, so I bought a variety."

Kendall scanned over the selection. "Ooh, Shrimp Lo mein—I'll pick this."

He chuckled under his breath as she dove into the carton with her chopsticks. It was then, he realized, that the way to Kendall Porter's heart was through her stomach. Her soft, feminine stomach.

Focus, Everitt. Take your mind off that beautiful body of hers—

"How did you manage to pull this off, huh? I thought it took at least a week for a campfire permit on the beach."

Ty shrugged. "I, uh, had a little help... Lana sort of moved my request to the top of the stack."

"Ah..." Lana worked at city hall as Mayor Cliffburg's secretary. One of Kendall's closest friends, Lana was also a valuable ally to have when you needed something accomplished at city hall quickly.

Ty popped the tops from two Corona's and fished two lime wedges from a Ziploc bag he'd unpacked from the basket. And after shoving the wedges into the bottles, he handed one to her.

"Looks like you've thought of everything."

Ty took a pull and then nodded. "Yeah, guess I've had plenty of time to think lately."

Kendall smiled at his choice of words. No doubt he was probably expecting a snappy comeback. In fact, she was sort of surprised the reprisal wasn't lingering on the tip of her tongue.

Wait for it, wait for it... Huh, that was strange. He'd anticipated a wisecrack, only it never came. Instead she simply smiled at him—which completely threw him off. Maybe she had a new tactic. Maybe she was trying to kill him with kindness.

Well, one thing was certain: she was killing him with that gorgeous smile.

"You okay?" she asked. "You look... *confused*."

"Probably because I am", he admitted as he stroked his chin. He studied her for a moment longer. "I was bracing myself for a jab."

"Well, I'm sure I can think of something", she offered lightly.

Ty chuckled. "I'm sure you could." Pushing the noodles around with his chopsticks, his expression turned serious. "I *did* put a lot of thought into tonight. I wanted to do something nice for you, you know?—without the worry of it becoming tomorrow's juiciest gossip."

Funny how a simple gesture could mean so much. Obviously, she enjoyed chatting amongst her friends about their lives, but unlike most women, she wasn't keen on "gossip." It'd always rubbed her the wrong way—even more so when she was the preferred topic of choice.

The fact that he took her feelings into consideration proved to Kendall that he did care. And that realization made her heart soften a bit. "You get me, Ty Everitt. You really get me... Thank you."

"You're welcome."

The crackle of the fire and the steady cadence of waves washing ashore swaddled them while they finished dinner. The combination seemed to lull him, soothe him. Or maybe his calm state of mind had to do with the alluring woman sitting to his left.

He took the opportunity to admire her while her eyes were closed for a moment. Kendall's skin was aglow as the flames reflected light against her bare shoulders, her black hair, the same color as the inky sky above, drifted effortlessly in the gentle Gulf breeze.

"You ready for dessert?" he asked, suppressing the urge to nibble on her delicious-looking lips.

And then those delicious-looking lips curved upward in a radiant smile.

"What did you have in mind?" she asked as she opened her eyes and settled them on his.

There was a number of ways he could answer that, but he kept silent. Reaching into the basket, he tossed the treat into her lap.

Kendall looked down. "A fortune cookie", she said flatly.

"Don't be shy. Go ahead. Open it."

Tearing into the plastic wrapping, she broke the brittle cookie in half, and then removed the small strip of paper inside. Clearing her throat, she read.

"ALL THE WATER IN THE WORLD CAN'T SINK A SHIP UNLESS IT GETS INSIDE."

She stared at the message for several moments and then took a bite of the crisp cookie. "Okay, so in other words: stay away from boats."

Ty laughed. "Guess that's one way to look at it!"

"Please tell me you're not one of those people who actually buy into this stuff", she uttered as she gestured toward the small paper.

"Sometimes you have to read between the lines, Doll. I think what your fortune is trying to say is, 'stay positive: don't let negativity bring you down.' "

"Then why not just say that, huh? Why use the whole 'sinking ship' metaphor?"

Ty shrugged his shoulders. "Don't know. Maybe the point is to stimulate your mind."

Kendall pulled her knees into her chest and leaned back on her hands. "Guess so. What does yours say?"

Snapping his cookie in half, he lifted the paper.

"AN ADMIRER IS CONCEALING HIS/HER AFFECTION FROM YOU..."

Ty glanced at Kendall. "Think there's any truth to *this?*"

Shrugging her shoulders, she repeated his words to him. "Sometimes, you have to read between the lines, Lieutenant. It did say *'his or her'*, didn't it?"

"So what are you trying to say?—some guy on the island has a man crush on me?"

"Anything's possible", she countered nonchalantly.

The sound of his laughter thawed the residual bitterness she felt toward him. He'd gone out of his way to make this night special, entertaining. Memorable.

Their playful banter seemed to remedy the tangled ball of nerves that'd settled in the pit of her gut, urging her to take a leap of faith.

Stay positive: don't let negativity bring you down...

She was going to follow her fortune (but still stay clear of boats). Because honestly, what's the worst thing that could happen?

Chapter 11

After tossing their garbage back into the picnic basket and refolding the blanket, Ty smothered the flames with a bucket of water and a few kicks of sand. Carefully, he led them back to his truck, loving how Kendall's orange blossom fragrance mingled with the salty breeze.

The evening had gone better than expected—like his two-week disappearing act had never happened. He appreciated the sentiment; appreciated the second chance he'd been given.

Tossing the blanket and picnic basket into the bed of his truck, he turned to her. "I have something for you." Although they were surrounded by darkness, he could still see the questions swimming in her eyes. "Hop in and I'll give it to you."

Ty opened her door and then hurried to the other side. Once he was seated behind the wheel, he flipped on the overhead light and reached in the back-seat.

Kendall eyed the wrapped gift and then met his gaze. "What's this?"

"Open it."

Hesitantly, she tore into the red paper, removing the lid, as well as the tissue paper neatly folded inside. She blinked several times, but never uttered a word.

"I, uh, saw you eyeing this the other day. Haven't been able to stop thinking about how beautiful you're going to look wearing it..."

Silence. And her expression: blank.

You fucking idiot!—now she probably thinks the sole purpose for tonight was to guarantee you'd get laid again.

Backpedal—FAST!

"Listen, you don't have to wear this tonight—I mean, I'm not implying something's going to happen between us again."

And then she looked at him. And it wasn't disgust or anger in her eyes.

It was shock and... *gratitude?*

"There's no hidden agenda here, Kendall. I just... wanted you to have this. You can decide when or *if* I get to see it on you."

Wow. She hadn't seen that one coming. Ty had completely blindsided her tonight. First with their quiet, secluded dinner, and then again with the pale pink bustier he'd purchased.

It wasn't about the lingerie—hell, he could've given her a jar of sand, for all she cared. It was the thought behind the action that astounded her.

She'd been on his mind.

Kendall was still looking at him, still silent. And then her body inched forward. *Hell, yeah—he was ready.* He licked his lips in anticipation as she palmed the side of his face. But when her lips were but a whisper away, she turned her head slightly, planting a peck on his cheek.

"Thank you... Thank you for thinking of me", she uttered softly as she pulled away.

"Sure." *If she only knew what he was thinking now...*

The ride back to Kendall's small Craftsman bungalow took roughly five minutes. During the drive, he thought about what'd happened. Or rather, what didn't.

She'd been close—so close—to kissing him, and for some reason had had a change of heart.

Not "some reason"—she's leery of your intentions. Of course she probably was. He hadn't exactly given her a reason not to be.

As soon as the truck rolled to a stop, Kendall opened the passenger door. His show of chivalry was nice—considerate—but it also left her feeling as though she wasn't in control.

And right now she needed to feel in control.

"Kendall—"

"Thanks again for tonight—for everything", she uttered as she carefully climbed down. *Just keep walking.*

Keep. Walking.

Her feet had barely reached the first step before the low rumble of the diesel engine quieted, followed by the sound of his door closing, and the steady thump of his footsteps as he stalked toward her.

"Lose something?" he asked.

Yeah—her manners, her courage, her mind.

Pick one.

"You forgot your purse", he declared as he handed it to her.

Kendall reached for her clutch and then met his curious gaze. "I'm sorry. Running off like that... it was incredibly rude of me."

Ty shoved his hands in his front pockets, afraid he'd reach for her. Afraid if he touched her again, he wouldn't be able to stop. "It's okay, Kendall. You don't need to apologize to me."

Their eyes met. Held. "You wanna come in?" she finally asked.

She was gnawing on that bottom lip again, something she seemed to do a lot when she was nervous. Vulnerable. Obviously she hadn't a clue what it was doing to him.

Nodding, he took the keys from her hand and opened the door.

"Can I get you anything?—beer, water?—a bowl of orange sherbet?" She called over her shoulder as she stepped inside.

Closing the door, he chuckled. "A beer would be great. Thanks."

Kendall went to the fridge, snagged a Heineken and returned to the living room. Ty was lounging on her gray sofa, his back comfortably pressed against an assortment of pillows, hands intertwined behind his head.

Confident. Enticing. Tempting. Just plain HOT.

His piercing green eyes tracked her as she approached, and then he flashed that flirty smile of his—the one that tended to liquefy her bones, causing her to literally melt.

And suddenly it occurred to her...

Forging ahead, she handed Ty the beer. "I'll be back in a minute. Just need to use the ladies room." Pivoting, she trekked down the hall to the guest bathroom, Ty's gift still clutched in one of her hands.

That powerful inner voice was at it again, although this time it wasn't whispering warnings, it was shouting them. She'd give that voice a stern talking-to later. Because right now, she didn't want to think. Right now she wanted to show Ty she could be exactly what he wanted: a fun, one-day-at-a-time kind of girl.

Removing her clothes, she quickly put on the pale pink bustier, slipped into the matching thongs, and then turned to the mirror. "You can do this", she whispered softly.

Kendall gave her reflection a once-over. And with a final nod of approval, she opened the door and stepped into the hallway.

Ty sat on the couch, noting the sway of Kendall's hips as she disappeared down the hall. He didn't deserve a second chance—not after the way he'd mistreated her—but he was going to take it. And this time, he wasn't going to fuck it up.

Kendall Porter was unlike any woman he'd ever met. Her ambition was fascinating, her forgiving heart was genuine, and her exotic beauty was enhanced even more so by her extraverted personality.

Kendall Porter was the whole package.

Maybe he had this all wrong. Maybe this *one-day-at-a-time* idea was hogwash.

Maybe—just maybe—he and Kendall had a legitimate shot...

Ty waited for the concept to send a shudder of fear down his spine—only it hadn't.

Huh. You're finally on to something, Everitt.

After a long swallow of Heineken, he started strategizing. Kendall needed to know he no longer wanted a one-day-at-a-time arrangement. Tonight he would tell her exactly what he wanted.

A real relationship.

Closing his eyes, Ty silently rehearsed his monologue, completely unaware that Kendall was standing behind him.

"I think it's time we had a little chat, don't you?" she asked softly.

Ty pinched the bridge of his nose and drew in a deep breath. "Yeah, there's actually something I wanted to talk to you about, too."

"Oh, yeah? Do tell..." She moved around the couch, finally coming to a halt in front of him.

"I was just thinking that maybe we—*holy fuck...*" He was dreaming—*he had to be dreaming*—because Kendall was standing less than three feet in front of him wearing the pink number he'd given her. His eyes trailed down her body, inch by glorious fucking inch, imprinting the image in his mind forever.

Kendall ran her hands over the satiny fabric, tracing the boning underneath. "It fits."

"Perfectly..."

His eyes perused her, her skin warming everywhere his gaze landed. "You were saying...?"

"What?"

"You were about to tell me something a second ago."

"I was talking?" he asked as he pointed to his chest?"

"Uh-huh."

Ty licked his suddenly dry lips and placed his beer on the end table. "For some strange reason, my brain's not working right now."

"Hmmm", she uttered as she stroked her chin.

"I've heard of this condition before." Stepping forward, she straddled his lap and proceeded to run her fingertips down the row of buttons on his shirt, over the ridges of his stomach, before settling on the bulge behind the fly of his jeans.

Ty hissed in a breath as soon as Kendall's hand began stroking him. God, she was killing him. Fucking killing him.

"It appears as though all the blood from your brain drained here."

Through hooded eyes, he stared into hers. The whiskey color was intoxicating, especially when they were glazed with desire. His hands traveled up her thighs, needing to feel her smooth skin under his callused fingertips. "You're the pharmacist—how do we fix this?"

"I'm sorry, Mr. Everitt, there aren't any drugs on the market to remedy your symptoms."

"No?" he asked.

"Huh-uh—although I do hear there's an experimental treatment your pharmacist can formulate. If you're interested..."

Slowly, her hips began to rock against him. Holy shit... "I'm all ears", he graveled.

"It's going to require placing the engorged appendage in a hot, wet environment."

Ty gripped her hips and groaned. "You know where I can find that?"

Kendall unveiled a mischievous grin and then leaned forward, pressing her lips against his throat. "Today's your lucky day, Mr. Everitt", she uttered as she spread kisses along his neck. "Just so happens I have one of those—"

"Damn it, Kendall, you're killing me!" He palmed

the sides of her face, ready to devour her, wanting to feel her slick tongue slide against his. Aligning their mouths, he prepared to do just that, but when they were but inches away, she placed her index finger against his lips.

"Uh-uh-uh—not so fast—first we have to lay some ground rules..."

"Ground rules?"

"Yes", she answered breathlessly. "Rule number one: the experimental treatment I've formulated must be repeated. *Often*—"

"—Think I'm going to like this treatment of yours—"

"—Rule number two: Once you've begun the experiment, you can't stop without first checking with your pharmacist. Three: It's still unknown how many treatments will be needed to fix the problem permanently. So I'll need your full cooperation—"

"—Anything you want", he groaned as he attempted to kiss her again.

Kendall pulled away slightly. "Good, because we'll have to take the treatments *one-day-at-a-time...*"

One-day-at-a-time? Did he hear her right?

So far he seemed to be on board, but there was still one thing left she needed to say. Because if she was going to engage in a no-strings-attached, physical relationship with Ty, she had to be sure he had no intention of making a similar arrangement with someone else. "Rule number four—pay attention, Mr. Everitt, because this is the most important one."

"I'm listening", he uttered, his voice so low—so gritty—it sounded as though he'd swallowed sandpaper.

"Once you've selected a location, you can't take your prescription to another pharmacy. Those are my

terms", Kendall announced as she leaned in to whisper
in his ear. "Shall I begin formulating your treatment
or do you need some time to think it over?"

Ty captured her face in his hands again. "Count
me in." He was done talking—the only thing he
wanted to hear was Kendall panting his name.

His mouth slammed into hers lustfully, aggres-
sively. And then he regained his composure, easing the
rhythm. The opportunity to taste her kiss again was
like receiving a priceless gift. One he vowed to savor
and cherish.

One he refused to take for granted again.

Lying next to Kendall on the kitchen floor, Ty's
lungs worked overtime as he struggled for oxygen.
They'd had sex—*hot, sweaty, amazing sex*—three
times. Once on the couch, then on the living room
floor, and finally the kitchen, where he'd taken her
from behind as she gripped the countertop.

And after satisfactorily coaxing her fourth—yes,
fourth—big "O" of the evening, he'd gathered her in
his arms, their bodies collapsing onto the wood floor
into a tangled pile of sexually-sated beings.

"So I take it I'm forgiven?" he asked as he ran
his fingers through her hair.

Kendall raised her head from his chest and smiled.
"You're forgiven." Who in their right mind could stay
angry with a man that good-looking? With that much...
talent? Pausing for a moment, she raked her teeth
across her bottom lip. "You know what I'm in the mood
for?"

"Geez, Kendall, we did it *three times*! We're gonna
run out of rooms soon." That earned him a playful

smack on the shoulder and another one of those adorable scowls she always exhibited when she was trying to appear mad.

"I wasn't talking about that", she corrected.

"Oh. What *were* you talking about, then?

"A half-gallon of orange sherbet"—she gestured with her fingers—"and two spoons."

Ty chuckled under his breath; he wasn't the least bit surprised. "You drive a hard bargain, Miss Porter", he disclosed as he swept a strand of hair from her eye.

"Yeah? I'm gonna run upstairs and grab my robe. I'll meet you back here in T-minus one minute."

"Deal."

Rising from the floor, they both scattered: Ty to the living room to find his jeans and Kendall up the stairs. And upon their return, they settled back onto the kitchen floor, the half-gallon container of orange sherbet between them.

Kendall marveled over the sequence of events that led to this point: a quiet campfire dinner on the beach for two, the lingerie, the bold decision to ignore her intuition... And now here she was, sitting on the floor sharing a half-gallon of orange sherbet with a half-naked man. Those ingredients equated to one hell of a Valentine's Day.

"So how do you think my first treatment went?"

Kendall thought for a moment. "I'd say it went very well—although your ailment is far from being cured. I get the feeling it'll take multiple, frequent doses before we begin to see any real progress."

Ty laughed, pointing his spoon at her for emphasis. "I like the way you think."

Kendall took a bite, savoring the cold, tart flavor on her tongue, finding comfort in the familiar tingle that settled deep within her jaw. "So what were you gonna tell me earlier?"

"Huh?"

"You know, earlier—before I interrupted you with my professional analysis... You said you wanted to talk to me about something."

His eyes settled on her beautiful face as he took another bite. "I honestly can't remember", he lied. "Guess it wasn't that important."

Yeah, you're full of shit, Everitt. You were moments away from telling her what you really wanted—to begin dating as a real couple.

Kendall's interruption couldn't have come at a better time. Because if he had confessed how truly infatuated he was with her, he would've only made a fool of himself. She wasn't interested in a relationship with him—she just wanted to be friends with benefits...

Funny how quickly things had changed. Two weeks ago he was worried about repeating past mistakes. Worried he'd find himself in the same position he'd been in with Cam: great sex, but no foundation outside the bedroom to build a lasting relationship.

And now the woman he shared a physical *and* emotional connection with only wanted him for sex.

But he wasn't giving up hope yet.

Nope, he'd go along with the *one-day-at-a-time* bullshit he'd initially suggested. For now. Because he planned to show Kendall Porter just how charming he could really be. And with time, she'd recognize that the deep connection they shared was far better than any fantasy she could conjure up.

Chapter 12

Sitting in Kendall's living room, surrounded by dozens of her closest friends, Olivia tore into her first gift. "Ooh, what do we have here?" she uttered as she gripped the large box. She tugged on the flap until the tape gave way and then gently unfolded the lid. "Omigod! Lana, this is beautiful!"

Olivia reached into the box and lifted the silver-frosted vase, holding it in front of her for everyone to see.

"I'm so glad you like it", she shared with a look of relief. "I know Grant has this whole *'coastal oasis'* thing going, and I figured this piece was a great fit—it's glitzy and glamorous without being too feminine."

"Well, I love it and I know he will, too. Thank you so much!"

"Are you writing this stuff down, Jenny?" Kendall asked.

Jenny gasped. "Thanks for reminding me!" She reached into her purse for a small pad of paper and a pen, preparing to document every gift Olivia received, as well as the names of the gift-givers.

Clutching a large glass pitcher, Kendall made her rounds, refilling empty glasses with the frozen watermelon daiquiris she'd concocted moments earlier. "Lana, can you start attaching the ribbons and bows to that paper plate sitting on the coffee table? The bride needs a bouquet for the rehearsal."

"Sure."

After Jenny successfully logged the first gift, she handed Olivia the next.

"How are the wedding plans coming along, Liv?" Lana asked.

"Pretty well, I reckon", she announced as she tore into the next gift. "Honestly, there wasn't much plannin' to do. We both agreed we wanted everything to be simple—I mean, I'm gonna be barefoot for heaven's sake!"

Olivia opened the second box, displaying a set of monogrammed, red wine glasses that everyone *oohed* and *aahed* over.

"Barefoot?" Jenny asked.

"Yes ma'am. The wedding and the reception are both being held on the beach." Olivia pointed to the group of women in the room, her finger scanning over the crowd in a sweeping motion. "And I expect everyone else to be barefoot, too, you hear?"

"So in other words", Kendall interpreted, "You better make sure you arrive with a fresh pedicure—no chipped polish or cracked heels allowed!" The women laughed. Satisfied that everyone had a full glass, she marched into the kitchen, placed the pitcher in the fridge, and then returned to the party.

"Well, I for one, think it's a great idea", Lana announced. "I was so uncomfortable on my wedding day. Couldn't even pee once I had my dress on—there was just so much tulle; I think I set the world record for the longest pee in one sitting that night! And if that weren't bad enough, the spaghetti straps nearly rubbed the flesh from my shoulders clear to the bone!" Laughter erupted from around the room again. "It's funny, you know?—you fantasize about your wedding day for years. And the only thing I can remember was my painful situation and how hungover Jimmy was from the night before! I can't even remember if the food was any good..."

"I'll save you the trouble"—Jenny interjected— "it wasn't. My prime rib was practically mooing on my plate!"

That comment seemed to amuse the crowd, although Kendall was too busy thinking about her future to join in the fun.

Her future. What a joke...

She was beginning to wonder if she'd ever be able to shake the restlessness she felt.

In fact, she had a terrible inkling she'd probably end up an old woman, still running Porter Pharmacy, selling denture cream and Preparation H to her peers. The highlight of her day: feeding the seagulls on the beach without being pooped on.

And let's not forget about her relationship with Ty. They'd most likely still be stuck in a *no-strings-attached* arrangement.

Okay, so that last part was mostly her fault. She agreed to the arrangement—even authored the terms—and had made sure to reiterate—often—that it was what she wanted, too.

It'd already been a month since they'd settled on the conditions—a monogamous, purely physical relationship, consisting of dinner, multiple orgasms, and an occasional dessert. And although their routine had become rather predictable, the sex wasn't.

They kept things in the bedroom... interesting.

Okay, so they rarely made it to her bedroom—but interesting nonetheless.

Sex with Ty was erotic, racy, dirty; the kind she thought only existed in the movies. But that's where the spontaneity ended. Because once their sexual appetites were fulfilled, they would fall into their normal routine: Ty would get dressed, kiss her on the forehead and say, *"Thanks, Doll. I had fun tonight."* And then he'd leave ...

"You okay?" Lana whispered as she crept up beside her.

"What?—oh, yeah—I'm fine." Kendall assured her. "Why wouldn't I be?"

"You just"—Lana shrugged—"look a little pre-occupied at the moment. Does it have anything to do with the pharmacy? I heard on the news earlier that another drugstore was robbed overnight near Apalachi-cola."

"Yeah, I heard that too. Luckily after we were targeted, I had a security system installed. It won't do much during business hours, but hopefully it'll deter anyone from breaking in when we're closed."

"So is that all that's bothering you?"

Kendall took a large gulp of her frozen daiquiri and attempted her best *everything-is-under-control* smile. "That's it", she lied. She turned her attention back to the bride-to-be, presently holding up a gift basket of assorted massage oils and other mis-cellaneous potions one would use for a long night of intimacy with the person they loved.

This charade was getting harder to carry out by the day. How much longer could she pretend that her arrangement with Ty was what she wanted?

How many days would she waste running her father's dream while ignoring her own?

Randall put his truck in gear, the island's lone fire station in his rearview mirror. He was exhausted, having spent the majority of the day training in full bunker gear. The warm early spring temperatures, coupled with the added seventy pounds of his air pack and heavy garb, made the mid-eighty degree temps feel more like a sweltering sauna.

It was Saturday: two-for-one's at the Oyster Saloon. And any other Saturday evening, that's where one would likely find him.

But not tonight.

After hours of running drills in the blazing sun, he'd showered, made a sandwich, and lounged in one of the many recliners situated in the corral of the station to catch the remnants of the Arnold Palmer Invitational on the tube. The tournament, held in Orlando, was in round three and the three-way tie for first place would've been riveting to watch if not for Kendall.

He could count on one hand how many times he'd seen her in the last month. She'd been on his mind constantly, but today her presence seemed to occupy every nook and cranny of his brain. And when seven 'o clock finally emerged, he threw his duffle bag over his shoulder and positioned his tired body behind the wheel, setting his sights on the pale yellow house on Third Street.

Randall wasn't certain she'd be home, but one thing he was sure of: tonight Kendall wouldn't be with Everitt. Ty would be holed up at the station till morning, giving Randall an opportunity to be alone with her for the first time in weeks.

Several minutes later, he parked his truck along the side of the street, noting that her Maxima was parked in the drive. His eyes scanned the yard, finally settling on the subtle glow behind the left front window. A shadow came into view, and although the two-dimensional figure could've belonged to any number of small-framed women on the island, he'd recognize that particular sultry silhouette anywhere.

Kendall.

Her shadow wasn't moving around much, and because he knew the kitchen sink was situated below the window, he figured she was most likely washing dishes. He sat motionless for several minutes, observing—thinking. And with a heavy sigh, reached for his phone.

With the bridal shower successfully behind her, Kendall set out to tidy her home. Several of her friends had offered to help—and she appreciated the gesture—but the neat freak inside her was practically writhing in anticipation as the final guest left her home.

The living room took minutes to complete—the area rug only needing a quick vacuum, and the throw pillows a good fluff, followed by a precise karate chop. She then carried the few dishes left behind into the kitchen to hand wash.

She'd been scrubbing away for some time, nearing the end of her clean up, when her phone rang. Removing her hands from the soapy water, she quickly dried them on a dish towel and reached to answer it.

"Hello."

"Hey, Babe."

"Hey, Rand—whatcha doing?" she asked as she sandwiched her phone between her shoulder and her ear, freeing her hands to finish the dishes.

Randall sat in his truck, his forehead resting against the steering wheel, his eyes clamped shut. "Well... right now, I'm sitting in front of your house."

Brushing the sheer café curtain aside, she peered through the window. "Why on earth are you doing that for?"

Lifting his head, he wiped his palm down the front of his face and chuckled—although nothing about his current situation seemed funny. "I don't know... Ah, shit, yes I do... Are you alone?"

"Yes."

"Mind if I come in?"

"Randall Wade Burns—I can't even believe you're asking me that—of course, you can!"

He hung up the phone and took in a hefty liter of air.

Keep the conversation light and easy. And whatever you do, DON'T TOUCH HER!

Chapter 13

Emerging from behind the wheel, Randall trekked toward the front door, and after letting himself in with the key she always kept hidden underneath the doormat, he strolled to the kitchen.

"Should've known you'd be cleaning," he greeted. "Wanna come back to my place?"

Kendall looked over her shoulder and smiled, quickly drying her hands. She walked several paces, embracing him in a friendly hug before pulling away. "Don't tempt me—you know I've been itching to organize your house for months! You thirsty?" she asked as she returned to the sink. "I have some leftover watermelon daiquiris in that glass pitcher in the fridge."

"*Daiquiris?*" he asked incredulously.

"Yeah, today was Olivia's bridal shower. That's what she felt like drinking, so I made a huge batch."

Randall slowly made his way further into the kitchen, coming to a halt directly behind her. He braced his hands on the counter, one on each side of her body, and kissed the top of her head. "Sorry, Babe, but men that drink pink slushies are pussies. Think I'll pass."

Kendall chuckled. "Guess you have a point."

Closing his eyes, he breathed her in and savored the sound of her laughter. It'd been almost a month since the last time he'd heard it. His chest suddenly became tight, his insides feeling as though they were on the verge of imploding. He'd convinced himself he was capable of keeping their aura light-hearted. But that innocent sound tugged at his heart in all the right places.

"I've missed that laugh", he uttered quietly.

"Rand—"

"What?—I'm not allowed to miss my best friend?"

Pivoting, Kendall turned to face him. "I've missed you, too... You've been somewhat of a hermit lately, you know?"

He nodded. "And you've been busy..." His gaze trailed down the contours of her face, finally settling over her mouth.

God, that mouth... What he wouldn't give to taste it—to feel it.

Unable to resist, he removed one of his hands from the counter and brushed the pad of his thumb down her bottom lip. The motion was slow and as he gently tugged on the plump surface, her lips parted.

"Rand", she whispered.

His eyes firmly locked on his intended target, he inched forward. Tilting her chin with his fingertips, his mouth brushed against her lips, a hint of sweet watermelon on her breath. And just when he thought she was about to give in, she turned her head.

"Damn it, Kendall..." His voice was soft, low—almost a groan—one he barely recognized as his own. "I love you. Let me show you how much."

Kendall peered into his gray eyes, noting the pain swirling in their depths. She hated that she was the one responsible for its presence; hated to see one of the most important men in her life in such agony. Allowing Randall to take her to bed would end his despair temporarily—yes—but then what? Affliction would soon resurface and they'd be back to square one all over again.

She'd do anything for this man. Lord knows he'd been there for her after her father's stroke. But this?—this she couldn't do. "It would never work between us, Rand."

"Why not?"

"Because..."

"Because you're not in love with me", he finished. "But maybe with time, you could learn to love me."

Kendall shook her head. "You deserve better than that—better than me."

"And what about you, huh? Ty's stringing you along like a fucking puppet, Kendall—he's playing you. *You* deserve better than that."

Stepping around him, she journeyed into the living room, aware that his footsteps followed behind. "You don't know anything about my relationship with Ty."

"Maybe not. But I know you—probably better than anyone... You're falling for him—"

"I am *not* falling for Ty Everitt", she declared.

"I sure as hell hope not. Because being tied down in a predictable, monogamous relationship is the last thing on his mind right now."

Kendall reached for the chenille throw that'd been precisely folded and draped over the arm of the sofa, and began refolding it. "And you know this because...?"

He watched her for a few moments. Clearly she was growing uncomfortable with the conversation. Her inability to remain still—fidgeting and re-straightening the already immaculately clean living room—proof. "Because I'm a guy. And if I were newly single after six years of marriage, commitment—of any kind—would be a non-negotiable subject. No way in hell would I let a nice piece of ass stand in the way of my freedom."

Kendall moved on to the pillows, re-fluffing them randomly to her liking. "Well, it's a good thing we're keeping things strictly casual, then. No promises. No emotions. No drama."

Randall flashed her the famous look: also known as his bullshit detector.

"What?" she questioned nonchalantly.

"C'mon, Babe, that's bullshit."

"Why?" she snapped as she placed one of her hands on her hip.

Randall braced his hands along the back of the couch, his focus on the black-haired beauty standing in front of him on the other side of the sofa. "Because women can't do no-strings-attached sex—can't do *casual.*"

Wrapping her arms around her middle, she answered, "Yes, they can."

"Okay—a select few can—but you're not one of them."

"Managed to keep that night last summer with you casual, didn't I?" Randall's expression hardened immediately, her thoughtless words diverging into malicious weapons. The moment they were spoken, she wanted to take them back. Her insensitive dig hung between them. And when he pushed away from the couch, shoving a hand in his front pocket, she knew she'd taken things too far. "Rand, I'm sorry. I didn't mean—"

Randall raised his other palm in front of him, cutting her off mid-sentence. "It's alright. I get it… I made love to my best friend that night. And to you it was nothing more than drunken sex."

She stood by as he turned to leave, overwhelmed with the need to smooth things over. "Rand, please don't go—not like this."

He came to a sudden halt after he opened the front door, looking over his shoulder one last time. "Be careful, Babe… just… be careful."

Eyes fixated on the closed door, she thought about what he'd said. *"Women can't do no-strings-attached sex—can't do casual."*

She could keep her emotions at bay. Because she was in complete control…

Grabbing her purse, Kendall hurried to her car.

Her destination: the fire station.

Her mission: substantiate how "in control" she truly was.

Ty sat in the kitchen of the firehouse, elbows propped on his knees, his hands supporting his head. The station was quiet, everyone having left over an hour ago. And as was usual these days, his mind drifted to Kendall.

They'd spent every night he hadn't been on shift together, satisfying their sexual appetites. And once their bodies were thoroughly sated, he'd retreat back to his place.

Alone.

The scenario was a single man's dream come true.

Only, now, it wasn't. Countless nights he would lie awake, his eyes boring holes in the ceiling, wondering if Kendall was lying in her bed thinking of him.

What he wouldn't give to lie next to her while she slept...

Frustrated with the direction his thoughts were leading him, he slowly ran both hands through his hair, sighing heavily as though it would somehow ease the tension expanding inside his body.

"Need to blow off some steam, Lieutenant?"

Ty's head snapped up at the sound of Kendall's voice. "What're you doing here?"

"Well, I was sort of hoping for an up close and personal tour of the fire truck. Know anyone around here that can help me with that?" she asked as she leaned against the doorjamb.

Rising from his chair, he slowly approached, examining the white cotton sundress clinging to her body. It looked heavenly—*angelic*—which was kind of ironic. Because the thin sheath had his mind swirling with all sorts of devilish ideas. The woman was just downright gorgeous, no matter what she was wearing— *or not wearing...*

Coming to a halt in front of her, he tugged on her waist, pulling her into his embrace. Nestling his face in the crook of her neck, he took a moment to breathe her in. The familiar orange blossom fragrance he began to identify with Kendall assaulted his senses immediately, silky black hair tickled his face, and the taste of her sweet skin had lust barreling through him at mach speeds.

"Today's your lucky day, Ma'am. I know just the man for the job. Follow me."

Intertwining their hands, Ty led Kendall through the main corridor, dashing through the heavy metal door that opened to the bay. They quickly meandered around the paramedic truck before finally coming to a halt in front of the large red engine.

Kendall was fascinated by the enormity. Sure, she'd seen this truck before plenty of times. But this was her very first up close glimpse. There were numerous compartments for various tools; knobs, gauges...

A sudden flash of heat settled low in her belly at the thought of watching Ty work, his large capable hands piloting the controls. His large capable hands caressing her body... "Are we alone, Lieutenant?" she asked as she leaned her back against the fire truck.

Ty stepped forward, bracing his hands against the truck on either side of her. "It's just the two of us." A sultry smile spanned her face, one that held wicked promises. But before he could dwell on its authenticity, she palmed the sides of his face and kissed him with unbridled urgency. And just like that, he was gone.

He was rabid for her. His body feverish, *burning*— overwhelmed with the need to embed his cock into her prime, willing body.

Guided by her whimpers, he lifted one of her thighs, grinding his hips against her warm center.

Kendall's hands roamed over his hard body as he ground against her, eventually settling over his belt, which she frantically unfastened. Reaching into his boxers, she gripped his hard length while his hips slowly pumped, foreshadowing the next act.

Ty's hands wandered to the apex of her legs, finding her panties moist. "Mmm, you're wet", he remarked hoarsely as he tugged them aside.

"You seem to have that effect on me."

"Is that right?"

"Yes", she whispered.

Still unhurriedly pumping into her fist, he uttered, "You know, I could probably get fired for what I'm about to do to you..."

Kendall nestled her lips against his ear, raking her teeth against his earlobe. "Guess it'll have to be our little secret, then."

God, he couldn't take it any longer. He cupped her sweet ass, lifting both legs from the ground, thrusting into her wet flesh. In the bay, up against the island's fire truck, he took her.

Hot.

Wild.

Spontaneous.

Physical.

Kendall was fully clothed, yet never felt so exposed—so naked—in her entire life.

He probed with deliberate, purposeful thrusts while his tongue nibbled and laved her neck.

"Omigod... Ty!"

Her inner walls contracted around him, the sensation feeling different—*good-different.* So good, his pleasure crested. His essence spilled into her throbbing core, each spasm siphoning every last drop. And at that very moment, awareness clobbered him: he wasn't wearing a condom.

Guess that explains why it felt "different."

"Please tell me you're on the pill", he inquired as his forehead thumped against the side of the truck.

Kendall nodded weakly. "I am."

Ty lowered her to the ground and wiped his palm down the front of his face. "I'm sorry. I never... we can't be careless like that again."

Kendall righted her dress. "Yeah, that wouldn't be good..." Yeah, no good. Because the last thing he wants is to be tied down to a woman he doesn't love and a baby he doesn't want.

"You okay?" he questioned softly.

Pasting a fake smile, she answered, "Of course... I should probably go before I get you into trouble."

Ty cupped her face, tilting it a bit so he could plant a peck on her lips. "Thanks, Doll. Don't think I'll ever be able to look at the fire truck the same again."

Kendall chuckled softly. "Yeah, me either." She saw something in his eyes—a flicker—something she'd never seen before. But as quickly as it'd surfaced, it was gone.

"Let me walk you out—"

"No, that's okay. I'll be fine."

"You sure?"

Kendall nodded, unable to find her voice. He planted another peck, this time on her forehead, and then she turned away.

Well, that tactic backfired...

She silently cursed herself as she returned to her car. The only thing she proved by coming here tonight: Randall was right.

She couldn't do casual, couldn't suppress her emotions.

She was falling for Ty. A man that had no desire to catch her.

Chapter 14

"I love you, Kendall", Ty said as he caressed her cheek. "I know this whole arrangement was supposed to be casual, but somewhere along the way, I fell in love with you."

"*Really*?" she questioned incredulously. "I-I love you, too. You don't know how hard it's been keeping that to myself!"

He smiled at her, his expression reflecting relief, happiness, and love. Her heart quivered at the sight.

Ty loved her.

"You know what this means, right?" he asked as he trailed kisses down her throat.

"W-what?"

"We have to sanctify this moment—honor it."

"And how do you suppose we do that?" she asked breathlessly.

"Think I have an idea..."

Ty grabbed a fistful of his shirt, removing it in one swift motion. His loving gaze settled on her, and then he kissed her. Slow. Tender. Lovingly.

* * * * *

Kendall's eye's opened wide at the sound of the doorbell. It took her a moment to get her bearings.

Damn. It was just a dream...

The doorbell rang again, prompting her to reach for her robe. Quickly, she wrapped it around her body and journeyed down the stairs.

Her eyes cut to the clock in the living room. She hadn't put on her glasses, but she was still able to make out the time: seven forty-five.

Unbelievable. The first day in weeks she hadn't scheduled herself to open the pharmacy and she still managed to be woken early.

Kendall yanked on the door, ready to give the inconsiderate asshole on the other side a piece of her mind, but paused when she came face to face with Barry Richardson, B.I.P.D. Chief. He was a tall, lanky man with graying hair and one of those mustaches that covered his entire mouth (a lip-reader's worst nightmare).

"Morning, Miss Porter. I apologize for disturbing you so early, but there's been a situation at the pharmacy."

"A situation...? You mean, another break-in?"

"No, not another break-in."

"Well, then, what?" she asked, confused.

"There seems to have been some...damage to the building. I'll need you to come with me to access the...uh, damages."

Kendall drew in a deep breath. "Okay, I just need five minutes to change."

There seems to have been some... damage. That phrase had replayed itself over and over in her mind from the moment it'd left Chief Richardson's lips (or mustache, rather). Her overactive imagination cooked up all sorts of possibilities. But as the Chief maneuvered the patrol cruiser onto Main Street, she had to admit the discovery was a bit of a shock.

The car rolled to a stop in front of the brick building that'd been home to Porter Pharmacy ever since her father opened for business over thirty years ago. She sat motionless for close to a minute, staring at the... damage.

"Know anyone that might have a grudge against you, Miss Porter?" Chief Richardson asked.

Kendall shook her head. "No."

"Okie dokie. Let's get out and have a look see, shall we?"

Nodding, Kendall emerged from the cruiser and stepped onto the curb. Who would do something like this? She wondered.

Spray painted across the large front window, in red capital letters were two words: FUCKING WHORE.

Just then, her pharmacy assistant, Marcus, caught sight of her and briskly approached. "There you are! I've called you about a hundred times this morning! Didn't you get any of my messages?"

Kendall closed her eyes briefly, recalling how she'd been so rattled after leaving the fire station last night, she'd left her phone in the car. "No. Didn't hear it ring... What happened?"

Marcus crossed his arms and shifted his weight onto one foot. "Well, I got here just after six-thirty to open. I parked in the back, so I didn't see anything at first. But as soon as I rounded the counter, I saw the... um... well, you know."

Kendall placed her hand over his forearm and gave it a squeeze. Marcus was a good man—had worked for her father for years. He was obviously uncomfortable with reciting the two words splayed across the storefront window.

"As soon as I saw it, I called you. And when you didn't answer after the first few attempts, I called the police."

"You did the right thing, Marcus", she assured him.

"Uh, Miss Porter"—Chief Richardson uttered as he joined the two of them—"it appears as though the culprit also sprayed the security camera you have mounted by the door. I'd like to take a look at the tapes. Maybe we'll get lucky and get an I.D."

"Sure", she answered. "Follow me."

Kendall led the Chief into her back office and rewound the tape. It took several minutes, but they finally came upon the crime. There was no sound, and the images were a bit grainy, but it was clear who'd been responsible for the damage: the two masked-men that'd robbed her at gunpoint several months ago.

The tape indicated they arrived just after midnight and had immediately realized that a security camera was recording their every move. The two masked figures appeared to talk for a few moments, probably discussing whether or not to take a chance on setting off an alarm, and then finally disappeared.

But the party wasn't over yet. The small masked-man in the baggy clothes came back about an hour later—alone—toting a can of red spray paint. He shook the can firmly, wrote his farewell message, then turned the spray can on the security camera.

"Well, we know how the vandalism unfolded, but the tape didn't give us any clues about who could've done this", Chief Richardson affirmed.

Kendall nodded her head and drew in a deep

breath. "So, now what?"

Chief shrugged. "Well, I'll have our detectives comb the entrance, although I'm not sure what good it'll do. In the mean time, you might want to get that security camera replaced."

"Will do. Thanks, Chief Richardson."

One by one the uniforms began disappearing, only to be replaced by curious residents that'd heard about the... damage.

Kendall was dumbfounded. Who was doing this? She was well-liked and respected in her small community. It just didn't add up.

She couldn't shake the feeling that the message left by the small masked-man was personal. *You're overreacting, Kendall. The guy was probably just pissed off that their plan fell through—probably hadn't anticipated on the small drugstore being newly equipped with cameras.*

Yes, that scenario seemed to fit better. The first time, there were no security measures in place and they most likely hadn't expected this time to be any different. Porter Pharmacy had been an easy target last time, and unfortunately it still was.

The cameras and a meager alarm on the back and front entries were all that stood between the intruders and their prize. And as soon as they figured that out, she knew they'd be back.

Grabbing her purse, Kendall walked across the street to the small hardware store in search of paint stripper and some razor blades. Her life was a complete mess—personally and professionally. Question was: what was she going to do about it?

* * * * *

"I can't believe you went back! I thought we agreed to stay away until we knew for certain how sophisticated the security system was."

"Oh, c'mon, Porter Pharmacy is nothing more than a podunk establishment in a gullible little town."

"Well, she was smart enough to install cameras, wasn't she?"

"The cameras are there for show—to deter anyone from breaking in. No way could she afford an elaborate security system. Aside from the cameras, I'd be willing to bet an alarm on the front and back door is about as complex as it gets."

"You're probably right, but I don't want to take any chances", he said as he crossed his arms over his broad chest. "There's a reason why I told you I never hit the same place twice... Going back again without me last night was an amateur mistake—"

"You're overreacting—"

"You better pray that's what I'm doing! Because if someone finds out it was you, I'll throw your ass under the bus. I'm not going down for your ignorance!" He took a step closer and lowered his voice for emphasis. "You're the one that convinced me to come back here. You better not fuck this up!"

"You're right—going back was probably careless. It won't happen again. I promise."

"Good. I'll wait several days and then head over there; assess the situation. Your little message no doubt has everyone on guard. We'll have to wait a few weeks before we make our next move."

"I'm really sorry."

"Do me a favor, will you? Lie low. I don't want you cruisin' around—just in case."

"Fine, I'll stay put."

Chapter 15

The day had finally arrived: Grant and Olivia's wedding day.

Kendall had spent the better part of the day at the beach house with the bride-to-be, lounging in the sun, chatting, painting their nails, while Grant and the best man hung out at Ty's.

When the late afternoon sun began its downward descent, the girls lined the make-shift aisle with tiki torches, covered the folding tables with white table cloths, and filled several large bins with ice to keep the beverages cold. The local barbeque joint was catering the event, and the owners, Mr. and Mrs. Lawrence, agreed to set up the food at no extra charge.

It hadn't taken long to get ready. After a quick shower, Kendall applied a light layer of make-up and straightened her shiny black hair. The strapless, knee-length bridesmaid dress she'd chosen was almost the same shade as her flesh, and the silky fabric hugged her curves like a second skin.

Olivia's wedding dress was simple: an understated, strapless sheath. No veil—just a modest-sized white flower tucked behind her right ear.

At sunset, roughly fifty of their closest friends and family gathered on the beach in front of Grant and Olivia's stilt home. There was no organ playing, no string quartet. When they emerged from the deck they were serenaded by the sound of the ocean and a flock of seagulls squawking as they soared nearby.

As promised, the ceremony was concise, quickly exchanging rings and *I do's*.

It was funny, really. Women often worked themselves into a tizzy, stressing over every minute detail from flowers to seating charts to the design of the programs.

Now don't get her wrong—those things were lovely. Kendall had attended numerous weddings that embodied elegance. But there was something refreshing about the understated simplicity of Grant and Olivia's nuptials that resonated with her. These two understood that their wedding day—although important—was merely a flicker in the span of their lives. They didn't want to look back on this day and recall being uncomfortable, forgetting how the food tasted, or if the music played on cue. They wanted to remember the promises they vowed, the amiable glances they shared, and the love they felt for one another.

Just before they were pronounced husband and wife, Grant gazed at Olivia. It amazed Kendall what that contented expression revealed: Olivia was North on his inner compass. And no matter how chaotic life became, he'd never lose his way as long as she was by his side...

The silent profession nearly stole Kendall's breath.

She wanted that. Wanted a man to view her as a precious gem, yet treat her like an equal partner. And as her eyes drifted to the best man, she realized if she wanted that, Ty Everitt wasn't going to be the one to give it to her.

The reception consisted of barbeque, beer, and a campfire, of course. An eclectic blend of tunes spewed from speakers along the raised deck, wafting through the airy evening, coaxing guests to sink their toes in the velvety sand and move their bodies in time with the beat.

Ty stood above the beach on the deck, elbows on the railing, his eyes glued to the raven-haired woman in the flesh-colored dress. Her hands were in the air, her hips swaying from side-to-side.

The woman was absolutely spellbinding.

Grant snagged two beers from one of the metal bins and perched his body next to Ty along the deck railing. His best man hadn't strayed from that spot since the reception began and as Grant eyed the crowd, he suddenly understood why.

"Here", he said as he handed Ty a brew, "you look thirsty."

"Thanks, man." He raised the bottle to his lips, letting the cool, frothy liquid slide down his parched throat. From his peripheral, he could see Grant staring at him with an amused expression. "What?" he finally asked.

Grant slapped him on the shoulder and gave it a firm squeeze. "You've got it bad, Bro."

Ty took another swig from his cool beverage, his eyes never swaying from Kendall. "Don't you have a wife to nag now?"

Grant smirked, releasing a soft chuckle. "Well, you're not denying it. So that must mean, I'm right."

Ty stole a quick glance at his new brother-in-law. "Go to Hell, Womack."

"Sorry, man—Hell's not on the honeymoon itinerary! Look", he began as his expression turned serious, "if you're that hung up on her, then... just tell her."

"Yeah..." It sounded easy enough. But what if she didn't feel the same way? What if she suddenly wanted out of their arrangement? Ty didn't want that. Because he was slowly beginning to realize that a lifetime spent with Kendall still didn't seem long enough.

The celebration was in full swing. Kendall had spent the majority of the reception on the dance floor—AKA: the sand—dancing with her girlfriends, belting out the lyrics to some of her favorite songs; only pausing long enough to refill her clear plastic cup with inexpensive chardonnay. Luckily the temperature had fallen into the mid-sixties upon nightfall and the constant coastal breeze prevented her from breaking a sweat.

Kendall had just emptied her third glass when the tempo slowed and large callused hands tugged her against a strong, broad body. "Hi", she uttered as she met Ty's smiling gaze.

"Hi." Ty adjusted their hands, his right loosely holding her left, while his free hand settled on the small of her back.

"I was wondering when you were gonna dance with me."

"I don't normally dance", he confessed.

Kendall pulled her head back and smiled. Breaking their hold, she ran her hands up his solid chest until her arms rested on his shoulders. "And yet, here we are…"

"You look like you're having a good time."

"I am. And you?"

His knuckles brushed against her cheek as his eyes bore into hers. "Watching you is always fun."

His voice was low, sexy. The tone sending shivers down her spine.

"You look absolutely beautiful, by the way", he commented.

"Thank you. You clean up pretty well yourself." Something was different, she acknowledged. She couldn't quite pinpoint what—it just… *was*.

"I was thinking… maybe we could head back to my place after the reception?"

"Your house." Her words came out more like a statement than a question.

"Yeah."

This was…*odd*. They never hooked up at Ty's—instead always choosing to fulfill their sexual appetites in the privacy of her cozy Craftsman bungalow (or parked along the deserted Northwest corner of the island in the cab of his truck or up against the town's fire engine). Never at his place.

She hadn't seen that one coming. "Um… okay."

Their bodies lingered, swaying silently until the song ended. And when the tempo accelerated again, he led her up the wood staircase to the deck for another drink. After pouring Kendall another glass of chardonnay and snagging another Heineken for himself, he gestured toward a more secluded section of the deck, away from prying eyes.

Kendall leaned against the railing and smiled, causing his breath to catch. Her black hair was whirling gently in the breeze. Unable to resist, he tucked a segment of the silk-like strands behind one of her ears. His gaze lowered down the contours of her face, down her throat, finally settling on two distinct points protruding through the fabric along her chest.

His fingers tingled at the thought of touching them; his mouth watered, envisioning the feel of her nipples on his tongue. He finally couldn't take it any longer. Discreetly, he brushed his knuckles against her chest, savoring her sudden intake of breath. "Either you're cold or really impressed with my dancing."

Kendall dropped her gaze to his hands as the backs of his fingers strategically swept over the front of her dress. She had to hand it to him—he was smooth. "Maybe a bit of both", she confessed softly. "I honestly didn't take this into account when I got dressed earlier. Guess that's what I get for going braless."

His knuckles trailed down her side, lightly caressing, tracing her silhouette as he spoke. "No bra, huh...? You're playing with fire right now. You know that, don't you?"

The low timbre of his voice had her insides twisting with anticipation. It still amazed her how Ty was able to do that to her—cause such a physical reaction by merely talking. "Guess I shouldn't mention that I'm not wearing any panties either."

Ty's mouth opened. His body froze. *No panties?* He'd been watching her all night, mingling, dancing, and all that time, she'd been carrying a secret. "Don't fuck with me, Ken..."

"I'm not."

"You're not wearing anything under that dress?"

he inquired again as he gestured toward the silky garment.

Kendall shook her head, then whispered, "No."

Groaning, he gripped her hand and headed indoors. "Get your purse."

"What?—why?"

"Because we're going back to my place."

"But—but the reception's not over yet", she reminded him. She dug her heels into the hardwood floor as he hauled her through Grant and Olivia's living room, attempting to slow him down a bit. But his steps never faltered. He wanted her. And his sudden loss of control had her mind spinning with naughty premonitions, her body flooding with sensual energy.

"It is for us."

Kendall managed to release his hold long enough to grab her purse and the small tote that contained her clothes and the toiletries she'd packed to get ready earlier for the wedding. When she came back to the living room, Ty met her with a devilish grin, one hand stuffed into his front pocket, the other held out for her.

"Let's go. I can feel the blood draining from my brain as we speak…"

Chapter 16

The drive to Ty's ranch-style home took under a minute, as he only lived five short blocks from Grant's beach house. Truthfully, Kendall expected Ty to jump her bones the moment they stepped foot inside—but he didn't. Instead, he calmly walked to the kitchen, snatched two shot glasses and a bottle of Jose Cuervo from the liquor cabinet, and filled each glass to the rim.

Kendall stood in the living room, scanning her surroundings, uncharacteristically nervous. Butterflies reveled in the pit of her gut as if it were her first time, which was completely absurd—she'd been intimate with Ty for almost two months now. Maybe it was her environment. Yeah, that had to be it. She was used to being with Ty in the comfort of her own home and—

"You gonna stand way over there all night?" he asked teasingly. Kendall smiled nervously as she drifted closer, finally halting beside him. She leaned her hip against the island and focused those exotic amber eyes on him. "Drink this", he ordered as he placed the shot glass in her grasp. Together, they raised the miniature glasses to their lips and tossed their heads back in a synchronized motion.

The tequila slid down her throat, leaving a fiery trail in its wake. She clenched her eyes shut as the blazing liquid burrowed lower, lower still, until the jittery flutter in her stomach was smothered.

"You okay?"

Kendall placed the glass on the island and opened her eyes. "Yes."

Ty stepped in front of her and pinned her body against the kitchen island. His intense gaze was penetrating as it swept over her. Slow. Steady. Thorough.

His knuckles brushed along her jaw, over her chin to the other side, before cupping the back of her neck. Lazily he inched forward, kissing the corner of her mouth. Her eyes fluttered, then closed as he ran his tongue along the seam of her lips, ending with a soft kiss when he reached the opposite corner.

"God, Kendall, what you do to me", he whispered against her mouth. He wanted to taste her—had to have her now—and when her lips parted slightly on a sigh, he took advantage, sliding his tongue between them.

His lingering kiss was slow.

So. Very. Slow.

She'd never been kissed like this—not by any man—certainly not by Ty. It was sensual, meaningful, and... confusing. Suddenly she felt discombobulated—completely out-of-place. Everything about tonight was different: their location, they way he looked at her, touched her, kissed.

Losing her grasp on control was a rare phenomenon—well, at least when it came to her personal life, that is. This was just... *too much*. In an attempt to regain command of the situation, her hands journeyed to the growing bulge behind the fly of his khaki's. Her mission was simple: speed things up. Because his slow, savory kisses allowed her mind to wander, allowed her heart to engage, and she couldn't let that happen.

What you and Ty have is purely physical. Just sex. Thinking it was anything different was dangerous.

Her palm brushed against his fly for a nano-second before he gripped her wrists and broke the kiss. "What're you doin'?" he groaned as his forehead came to rest against hers.

"What you brought me here to do." She tried once again to feel him, but his grip tightened.

"Stay", he whispered.

"This isn't going to work if you won't let me touch you—"

"I don't want to rush tonight. Stay... Spend the night with me..."

"Ty", she sighed, "that's not a part of our agreement. We both—"

"Fuck the agreement. Rules were meant to be broken." He tasted his way over her chin, down her throat. "I want to take my time—taste every fucking inch of you..."

This is a bad idea! Sex is one thing—spending the night in his bed, lying next to him is too intimate. Don't do this! The voice of reason bellowed its warning. She should listen—

"Will you?" he graveled against the crook of her neck.

Could she? Could she spend the night with the man she was falling in love with and wake the next morning with no regrets? Avoid the awkwardness of the morning after? "Yes", she whispered.

His lips shifted away from her neck as he took her by the hand. He led Kendall down the hall until they came upon the last door on the left. His heart hammered against his chest as he guided her into the master suite. He stole a quick glance at her over his shoulder as they entered. Her steps were cautious and her expression was demure-like. He wondered what she was thinking...

Kendall had traveled down this hallway hundreds of times growing up. She and Olivia had been practically inseparable.

But she'd never been in the master suite before—until tonight.

With the flip of a switch, fifteen years of mystery was suddenly unveiled.

Ty turned on the lamp beside the bed, casting the modest-sized room in a soft, intimate glow. The large bed was framed in sleek espresso wood, a bold contrast against the beige walls. A burnt-orange comforter was haphazardly spread across the king-size mattress as though he'd been in a hurry (although the fact that he attempted to make his bed at all was a pleasant surprise). At the foot of the bed, a load of fresh folded laundry lay on an ivory upholstered bench.

The space was actually rather neat for a bachelor pad—no dirty underwear or sweaty socks lying on the hardwood floor, no repulsive odors. In fact, the room smelled like Ty: a mixture of woodsy soap, designer cologne, and confident masculinity.

Fifteen years...

And just like that, she was reminded of the woman that'd shared this bed with Ty. Maybe being here wasn't a good idea after all.

"You okay?" he asked as he came up behind her.

"You look tense." Ty brushed her hair aside and kissed the back of her neck.

Kendall moaned as goosebumps temporarily marred her smooth skin. Lower, his lips moved until he came upon the top of her dress. Slowly he tugged on the zipper, the separation of metal links and her heavy breaths the only sounds.

She should stop him—explain the uneasiness she felt. Disclose that being in the room he'd made love to his ex-wife in for the past six years made her... uncomfortable. But, God, the things he was doing with his mouth felt so good. His lips trailed a path down her spine, chasing the zipper as he idly drew the small metal tab down her back.

Closing her eyes, she pushed the images aside. She wanted this—wanted this man—and she was going to have to trust that when Ty looked at her tonight, he wasn't envisioning a short blonde woman with medically-enhanced double Ds.

Kendall's aromatic skin was heavenly. A mixture of delicate orange blossoms and fresh coastal breezes. Her stiff muscles softened as his lips journeyed lower. And by the time he reached the small of her back, her body was blooming with eagerness.

The dress slid down her bare body with a little help from Ty and lay in a puddle around her perfectly pedicured feet. Spreading soft kisses over her shoulder he asked, "Do you trust me, Kendall?"

"Y-yes."

Her admission made his chest squeeze. *She trusted him*... Tonight he wanted to show her how good it could really be. Wanted to prove their attracttion went beyond "physical." Wanted to convince Kendall that it was time to renegotiate the "terms" of their so-called one-day-at-a-time arrangement.

"I want you to lie face down on my bed", he murmured as he unbuttoned his white shirt. Her steps were hesitant at first as she moved away from him. Something had her distracted. His soft kisses had eased the tension from her rigid muscles, but he'd yet to quiet her thoughts. Obviously her mind was still elsewhere.

That was okay—for now. Because by the time he was finished with her tonight, she would finally know how crucial she'd become in his life.

Ty shrugged out of his shirt just as Kendall climbed onto his bed, slowly crawling on all fours until she reached the center. The view from his standpoint was heavenly, decadent. She unhurriedly lowered her lean body onto the mattress. "You did that on purpose", he uttered as he retraced her steps.

Kendall looked over her shoulder and smiled. "Maybe..."

The mattress shifted as he placed each of his knees on either side of her body, straddling her legs. His large callused hands traveled up the backs of her thighs before settling on the bed next to her head. He swooped down, his lips sweeping against the back of her neck again. And as promised, he kissed his way down her body, veering occasionally in an attempt to target every erogenous zone.

The soft tickle of his lips, the slippery sensation of his laving tongue caused liquid warmth to pool between her legs. And when he kissed the backs of her thighs, she whimpered and wriggled in delight. Never had she felt so cherished. "Ty..."

"Yes, Doll", he whispered against her hip.

"*Please...*"

She was begging him. And as much as he wanted

to give in—to give her exactly what she was pleading for—he held back. For the past two months, their fiery chemistry had caused them to be adventurous—even reckless at times. Sex with Kendall was exciting, daring. Hot as Hell. They were like magnets when they were alone together—drawn to one another immediately. It'd always been hard to separate—leave her at the end of the night.

Tonight he didn't have to. He had all night to feast on her body. And that's exactly what he planned to do. "Turn over", he commanded softly.

Bit by bit, Kendall turned underneath him until she was lying on her back. He hovered above her, his eyes at half mast as they settled on her. They raked across her body, lazily taking her in. There was something incredibly erotic about it—she was completely naked, and aside from the shirt he'd removed moments earlier, he was fully clothed. It was unsubstantial, really. But something about it turned her on.

His mouth gradually found its way to her lips. The tenderness nearly stole her breath. Ty kissed her as though she were the most precious thing in the world. As if she was special.

As if she truly mattered.

Although her eyes were shut, the immense feelings she garnered for this man, coupled with his warm gentle touch, inspired tears to leak from her closed lids. His sensual kisses ventured down her chest, temporarily veering off-course to greet each eager nipple with his mouth. He continued down her taut, feminine stomach, causing her belly to tremble.

Ty couldn't ignore the irony. He had Kendall pinned beneath him. Outwardly he appeared to be the one in control.

But he wasn't—not by a long shot. He was at Kendall's mercy.

The painful pressure of his hard length bulging behind his fly was irrelevant at the moment. Watching Kendall's body react to his touch was all that mattered. So far, he'd managed to stay clear of the treasure between her mile-long legs, wanting to draw out their foreplay for as long as possible. And now it was time.

His hands settled between her legs, finding her unbelievably wet. His fingers delved between the folds, and when he found just the right spot, he hooked his finger in a come-hither motion and stroked. Firm. Slow. Unable to curb the craving for this woman any longer, his mouth came down on her.

The sensations he inflicted were otherworldly—so damned divine—she almost forgot to breathe.

"Love the way you taste, Doll", he uttered gravelly.

Ty continued—his tongue swirling, licking—his lips suckling, kissing—his fingers fondling, caressing. She was sinking deeper, gasping for breath, her hands gripping his hair, desperately clinging to stability as her world was spinning.

"That's it, baby—let go."

The spark ignited from deep within, quickly expanding until her insides were ablaze. Her body writhed, fanning the internal flames until she was completely engulfed in red-hot pleasure.

And as her feverish body tempered from the searing summit she hurdled over, she could no longer deny: she was in love with Ty Everitt.

Madly. Deeply. In love.

While Kendall was still in the midst of coming down from her climax, Ty reached into his back pocket for protection, quickly losing his pants and gaining a thin sheath of latex. He came to rest beside her on the bed, pulling her in close, anchoring her body against his solid chest.

This was too much. Everything pressing in on her all at once. She loved Ty. And now they were locked in a loving embrace. *You need to regain control of the situation and yourself!*

Yes, she did. She needed to snatch the reins from Ty's grasp and commandeer the remainder of the evening. Rolling him over on his back with authority, she rose above him and straddled his lap. She reached between them and gripped him, aligning their bodies. She felt the latex against her palm—when had he done that?

Probably around the same time you realized you're head-over-heels.

With the tip of his sex in position, she lowered her body, inch by glorious inch until her bottom sat fully against his lap. He drew in a breath through clenched teeth as she placed her palms against his chest, her body rising, then falling, her repetitions becoming harder. Faster.

This was better. The rapid and powerful motion was normal. Comfortable. Like all the other times.

But it didn't last.

Moments after she'd established a hasty rhythm, his strong hands dug into her hips, ending her unbridled ride.

He knew what she was trying to do. She was trying her damnedest to run the show, and normally he'd let her.

But not tonight.

In one swift motion, he turned, pinning her body against the mattress. His movements were slow, deliberate, each thrust meant to emphasize how passionately he loved this woman.

Love.

That four letter word should've delivered a frightening jolt of fear down his spine. Only it hadn't. Somewhere between one-day-at-a-time and observing the soft sway of her hips on the beach earlier tonight, he fell in love. He'd fallen for Kendall Porter like a stone through the clouds. Hard. Fast. And he never wanted the freefall to end.

"Don't close your eyes, Doll", he whispered as her lids fluttered. "Look at me—*feel me*", he groaned as he plunged into her again.

Sex with her lids open, staring into the eyes of the man she loved, sharpened every sensation. And when he reached between their bodies and swept his thumb over her sensitive flesh in soft lazy circles, she surrendered to the physical, and emotional, stirring that'd settled deep in her core.

Her slick inner walls clamped down around his sex, pulsing as though they'd come to life, the steady cadence like a strong heartbeat. Her body gripped, then released—over and over—forcing his body into a similar sequence of surging energy. Ty cursed as his essence fled his body, spilling into the latex barrier. He couldn't recall a time he'd felt so fulfilled—like everything he'd ever need was right here, staring back at him.

This time was different than all the others—he couldn't refute what he was feeling. Nor did he want to. He'd tell her how he felt tonight.

But not now.

Kendall was his until dawn. And he intended to make every second count until then.

Chapter 17

Two hours—and several orgasms later—they collapsed onto the mattress, their legs tangled, Kendall's head resting against his chest. Questions plagued Ty's mind (or maybe it was the answers to the many questions). Had tonight been different for her too? Had the impassioned look in her eyes been love?

God, he wanted to believe so.

He was so tired of pretending—tired of acting as if his breath didn't catch every time he looked at her.

His fingertips incessantly swept up, then down her arm as his mind worked to solve the mystery. Finally overwhelmed with the unknown, he decided to delve into the truth. "What're you thinkin' about, Doll?"

"That's a very *chick* thing to ask", she replied with a hint of amusement.

Ty laughed. "Yeah, I guess it is... *So...?*"

"You *really* want to know?"

He hesitated for a few moments. *Did he?* Did he really want to know? Was he prepared to hear the truth? They were loaded questions. But, yes, the suspense was killing him. "Yeah."

Kendall inhaled a deep breath. "I was just thinking about the future."

Okay, that sounded promising. "What about it?" he probed.

This was so hard. The words lingered on the tip of her tongue, but somehow saying them aloud made everything seem... *real*. She needed to just blurt it out—get it over quickly. Like ripping off a Band-aid. "I was thinking about... *not* renewing my lease at the end of next month."

Okay, he wasn't expecting that—but this was still good news. Wasn't it? "Looking for more square footage?"

"Not exactly... Just before Christmas, I applied at a pharmacy in Jacksonville. And...two days ago I was offered the position. It's just part-time, for now— until I can find a replacement for myself here at Porter Pharmacy. But at some point, it would become full-time."

Ty's hand halted in mid-caress as she shared the specifics about her plan. *She was planning to leave...* The realization blindsided him. Of course he knew she'd only come back to Butler Island two years ago because of her father's stroke and had always wanted to distance herself from the constant meddling that resulted when one lived in a small town.

Kendall and Olivia were alike in that way—one of the many reasons why they were best friends. They had both gone away to college; had experienced what it was like to reside in a big city. Kendall's intentions never included staying in Butler Island long term. In the back of his mind he always knew that. But he'd hoped that their relationship would've changed her willingness to leave.

You're a fucking fool, Everitt! This has always been a no-strings-attached relationship. She always planned on leaving. You were just pleasurable entertainment until that day arrived.

"What do you think?" she finally asked. Kendall raised her head from Ty's chest, looking into his eyes for any visible signs of emotion.

Ty shrugged his shoulders in an attempt to appear at ease. "I think... you should do whatever makes you happy."

"That's not what I asked you."

"What do you want me to say, Ken?"

Stay. Tell me not to go. "Nothing. Just forget I mentioned it", she uttered quietly.

Their bodies lay motionless for some time, the soothing hum of the ceiling fan whirling above the only sound.

She didn't love him—that much was now obvious. He'd fallen for an emotionally unavailable woman. A raven-haired, ambitious beauty whose career mattered more than he ever would...

Ty glanced at the clock on the nightstand: it was after three. He should be tired; it'd been a long day. But he couldn't sleep—not while his mind was trying to process the bombshell she'd unloaded.

He listened to the slow, steady cadence of her breaths. She was asleep—completely unaware that her confession had caused him such turmoil. Carefully, as not to wake her, he slipped out of bed and reached for his boxers. He needed something to dull the ache in his chest and a shot of tequila—maybe two—was the likely choice.

After slipping into his underwear, he shuffled into the kitchen and filled one of the shot glasses to the rim. Painstakingly, he brought the small container to his lips and closed his eyes as liquid heat slid down his throat. The tequila burrowed deep, settling in his gut, soothing him from the inside out.

She was planning to leave. Soon.

Ty was certain her loving gaze revealed how she truly felt about him tonight. Surely he hadn't imagined that. Or had he? Was he so far gone for Kendall that he detected only what he *wanted* to see, instead of what was really there?

Unable to stomach the cold hard truth, he poured another round and doused his new reality with an anesthetizing potion before finally returning to his room. Kendall was sound asleep and so damn beautiful lying in his bed.

Take a mental picture. Because soon her presence here will be just a distant memory.

Lying on his side next to her, he watched Kendall sleep. Silky strands of black hair spilled onto the pillowcase, surrounding her angelic face like a dark halo. She looked... peaceful (at least one of them was). The comforter had slid down her body, revealing the darkened border of her left nipple. A part of him wanted to wake her and feast on her heavenly body again. But he ultimately decided against it.

Instead he observed—witnessing the rise and fall of her chest as she breathed—etching a permanent place for Kendall's flawless form in his memory bank.

As if she sensed his thorough examination, her body shifted, burrowing closer to his chest. Ty couldn't help but think how perfectly her body fit against his. Closing his eyes, he scolded himself. He and Kendall wanted different things. She wanted to blend; live a life where her discretions and choices didn't matter to her neighbors. And Ty?—well, he was beginning to think the only thing he really wanted was to matter— to her.

"Well, *this* is certainly a surprise..."

Ty stirred a bit, wincing as bright light beamed through the slats of the wood blinds. Even with his eyes closed, the intensity caused his aching head to painfully pulse. Fearing his brain would explode from the blinding morning light, he cautiously opened one lid—just a sliver—allowing his vision to adjust to the vivid glow. But one tiny peek suddenly made his eyes go wide with astonishment.

Because standing at the foot of his bed with arms crossed was none other than his ex-wife.

"What're you doing here?" he questioned as he carefully slid his arm from underneath Kendall's body. Ty sat up and glared at Cameron, the motion causing Kendall to stir as well.

Kendall opened her eyes, taking a moment to gather her bearings. It took several seconds for her to realize that she was in Ty's bed (and several more to realize that they had company). Gasping in surprise, she instinctively covered her body with the orange comforter, clutching the soft microsuede for comfort.

"I need to talk to you", Cameron explained.

"You could've just called, Cam. *Jesus,* how did you get in?" She dangled a set of keys in front of her as Ty scrubbed his palm down his face. "Time to change the locks", he muttered wryly.

This wasn't happening, Kendall thought. It was a bad dream—had to be a bad dream. Because this couldn't really be happening! "Um, I think I should go", Kendall uttered softly, barely able to form the words.

"Yeah", Cameron spat.

"No", Ty defended simultaneously. He sighed in frustration. "Damn it, Cam, what could we possibly have to talk about?"

Cameron's eye's shifted to Kendall, then back to Ty. "It's... *personal.* I'm staying just over the Mainland Bridge at Bayside Cottages—unit twelve. When you get a spare minute, stop by." She turned to leave and then stopped just short of the door, looking over her shoulder at Kendall. "I wouldn't get too comfortable, honey. Ty prefers blondes."

The drive back to Kendall's house was silent and thick with tension. She hadn't uttered a word since Cameron's departure. As soon as they were alone, she'd quickly snatched her bridesmaid dress off the floor and barricaded herself in his bathroom for twenty minutes.

Obviously she'd been caught off-guard by Cameron's sudden arrival—it was pretty safe to say both of them had. What man would knowingly bring a woman home to bed with the expectation that his ex might drop in? None that he knew of. Damn it— Cam had impeccable timing...

After Kendall opened the door, she nervously tucked a strand of black hair behind her ear and settled her gaze on the floor. *"Please, take me home",* she'd managed just above a whisper. And without looking at him, she grabbed her purse and headed to his truck.

Kendall deserved an explanation. But truthfully, he didn't have the slightest clue why Cam had come back. Minutes after backing out of his driveway, they arrived at Kendall's. Shoving the gear into PARK, he turned toward her. "Kendall—"

"Thanks for the ride", she stated as she pushed the door open. "Guess I'll see you around..."

And just like that, she was gone. He sat motionless in his truck as she scurried up the steps and uncovered the key hidden underneath the doormat. Ty closed his eyes and allowed his head to rest against the seat. He hadn't imagined it—the look in her eyes last night was hopeful. And today? Today she couldn't even stand the sight of him.

Ty released a heavy sigh and opened his eyes. The front porch was empty; Kendall was already inside. He knew things wouldn't revert back to normal until he unearthed the reason behind Cam's surprise appearance.

And that's precisely what he planned to do next.

Chapter 18

Bayside Cottages was situated on the mainland along the coast. And on a clear sunny day, one could absorb the sun's brilliant rays while taking in a panoramic view of Butler Island's secluded Northwest shore. Palm fronds danced in the steady breeze, whispering and stirring, although the sound was partially muted by the clamor of his rapid pulse.

Ty pounded on the door of unit twelve with his fist and then took a step back. This is not how he planned to spend his morning. He should be back at home—in bed—with a certain pharmacist. Should have been buried deep in her body. Every hot-blooded man in the world knew that morning sex was the best. Men woke up ready. Eager. And because the male species were visual creatures, the dazzling glow from the rising sun provided an up close and personal view of the lovely female form.

The door opened, revealing a smiling Cameron. "You came", she uttered, the tone of her voice beaming with enthusiasm and hope. She opened the door wider and stepped aside, motioning for him to enter.

Ty stepped inside and surveyed the small unit. He couldn't recall the number of times he'd passed this place since its construction roughly ten years ago. Too many. He'd never actually been inside one of the cottages before, though—never had a reason to be.

Until now.

Although the cottage was small, it encompassed all the comforts of home. The living area was only capable of housing a loveseat, a wicker chair, and a small TV resting on a narrow white console. The kitchen seemed rather claustrophobic—in fact he doubted two adults could occupy the compact space at the same time. But what the cozy cottage lacked in square footage, it made up for in style. The beach theme was understated, soothing—not at all like the countless corny hotels one might encounter along the Florida coast.

"Can I get you something to drink?" Cameron offered as she shut the door.

"Not necessary. I don't plan to stay long."

"You look good", she offered.

No matter their past, he couldn't deny that she looked good too. Cameron was a beautiful woman. Her long golden locks had grown substantially since the last time he'd seen her, settling just below her double Ds. The yellow sundress tied around her neck enhanced her deep cleavage and the clingy fabric hugged her hourglass figure perfectly.

But looks weren't everything.

Cam's manipulative nature, although camouflaged well behind her fine exterior, was her Achilles' heel.

With his weight distributed on his left foot, he placed his hands low on his hips and glared at his ex-wife. "Cut the small talk, Cam. What're you doing here?" he inquired impatiently.

Cameron took even strides toward him, stopping mere inches from his broad masculine body. "I miss you." Raising her gaze to his handsome, unshaven face, she gauged his reaction... Nothing. No emotion what-so-ever.

Placing her palms against his stomach, her hands swept upward until she reached the solid wall of his broad chest. She rose onto her toes and placed her lips against the hollow of his throat as she spoke. "We were good together, Ty. You remember how good it was, don't you?"

There was a time in his life when the touch of her small hands on his body and the sensation of her mouth on his neck would have brought him to his knees. But now? Now he felt zilch. Peeling her hands off his chest, his eyes bored into Cameron's. "I remember coming home from shift to find your wedding ring and a fucking farewell letter."

"I'm sorry, Ty. For what it's worth, I never meant to hurt you", she confessed softly.

"Well, it's a little too late for that, don't you think?"

"No", she affirmed as she shook her head. "Look, you asked why I came back... I want things to go back to the way they were. Before we... before *I* screwed up."

"That's the understatement of the century", he mumbled wryly.

"You're still angry with me—I get that. And I deserve it. I betrayed your trust—our vows—and took you for granted... You know that old saying, *'the grass always looks greener on the other side?'* Well, when I met Jeff, it did. He was everything I thought I wanted. But I was wrong... I want to make our marriage work."

Ty started for the door. "It's too late. I signed the papers—it's a done deal."

"Not exactly..."

Those two words halted him in his tracks. *This* was the Cameron he knew: the conniving and manipulative woman that stopped at nothing to get what she wanted. His body cringed as he turned around to face her. "What did you do...?"

"Actually", she said as she slowly trekked toward him, "it's what I *didn't* do... I never filed the divorce documents. So 'legally' ", she announced as she made quotation marks with her fingers, "we're still married."

Ty closed his eyes, whispering a sequence of four-letter obscenities. And when he finally opened them his vision was clouded with unadulterated rage.

"And since technically we've *both* been unfaithful, I'd say we're even", she clarified as she twirled a segment of her long blonde hair around her index finger.

"Have you lost your fucking mind?"

"No. In fact, I've never been more clear-headed in my entire life. I want to make this work, Ty. And I know we can if—"

"You're delusional. Fucking. Delusional", he managed through clenched teeth.

"Really?" she began, her incredulous tone laced with amusement. Crossing her arms, she took a step forward and tilted her chin, looking her husband in the eyes. "Let me ask you something, Ty. Are things *serious* between you and Kendall? Huh?"

"My relationship with Kendall is none of your God damn business!" A smile spread across Cameron's lips—and not a pleasant one. No. *This* smile was... devious.

"We're still married, Ty—*of course,* it's my business." Cameron allowed her gaze to wander over him. His brows were drawn, two green eyes swirled with rage, and his jaw was set. Anger rolled off his solid body in waves, but there was something else, too: Panic. And suddenly everything began to make sense. "You love her, don't you?"

Ty wiped his hand down his face, trying his damnedest to regain his composure. He needed to get out of this room. The walls were closing in on him. Turning away from her, he reached for the door. "I have to go."

"I think you've got it all wrong, Ty. *You* are the delusional one. Kendall Porter came back because of a family crisis. She may've grown up here, but she's a city girl at heart. In fact, I wouldn't be surprised if she already has one foot out the door!" Taking several steps forward, she gripped his upper arms and pressed her breasts into his broad back. "She can't appreciate you—not the way you deserve", she whispered.

"And you can?" he shot back scornfully as he looked over his shoulder.

"Yeah, I can. Because I've done the whole 'big city' thing. And none of it was as good as being with you. Listen, I don't want you to give me an answer right now. Just... *think about it.*"

Think about it, my ass! Ty couldn't believe this was happening. Well, on second thought—yes, he could. This kind of stunt was right up Cam's alley. She was a master manipulator—always had been. It'd just taken six fucking years of his life to realize it!

Honestly he should've known better. Should have known she was up to something. He'd sat on those divorce documents for roughly three months—divorce documents she'd initiated—without one harassing phone call on her end. Sort of made him think she had no intention of ending their marriage in the first place.

Yep. He was beginning to understand the specifics of her plan.

His wife willingly spread her legs to a stranger and then had run off with him. She filed for divorce—leading Ty to believe she had moved on. Meanwhile, she indulged in a sexual adventure. And when the thrill was gone, she was confident that Ty would simply welcome her back with open arms...

Damn it—what had he ever seen in that woman?

Double Ds, a tight little body, and a hungry sexual appetite. Yeah, it was all coming back to him now: he'd been thinking with his cock.

Ty was in love with Kendall Porter. And still married to Cameron.

Fuck!

Kendall was going to flip when she got wind of this!

Lying beside her last night felt right—like they were both exactly where they were supposed to be. Together.

Maybe Cam was right—you are delusional. Kendall is making plans to leave Butler Island, remember?

He needed time to think. Needed time to calculate his next move.

Needed to figure out how he would break the news to the woman he loved.

It was a slow day at Porter Pharmacy. Kendall had already reloaded her stapler, reorganized her highlighters from lightest to darkest (again), and was currently aligning paperclips into a perfectly neat stack. A typical slow, OCD kind of day.

Exactly what she didn't need. Because when business was slow, her mind wandered.

It'd been two days since Ty had deposited her onto her driveway—two days since she'd spoken to him.

Two. Whole. Days.

His absence felt like déjà vu all over again. And just like last time, she didn't have a clue why he was suddenly avoiding her. Although she was certain that Cameron's unanticipated arrival probably had something to do with it.

Kendall had no claim on him; they had a casual, no-strings-attached arrangement. Cameron, on the other hand, had a history with Ty—a marriage. Maybe seeing her again made him realize he was still in love with her…

Stop it, girl. You'll drive yourself mad inter-preting what all of this means.

Yeah—too late for that.

"Excuse me. Do you have any larges in the back?"

Kendall's eye's drifted away from her newly or-ganized top drawer, to the box of condoms that lay in front of her on the counter, and finally settled on the woman that'd placed them there.

Cameron.

"Pardon?" Kendall asked, praying her voice hadn't trembled.

"I wondered if you had more stock in the back. This was the last box of larges on the shelf."

Kendall swallowed hard. "Uh, no. I'm sorry. We must be all out, then."

Cameron reached into her purse and laid a crisp twenty dollar bill on the counter. "You seem… *tense,*

Kendall. Maybe you should get laid or something", she punctuated.

Kendall chuckled under her breath, although she wasn't the least bit amused. *Stay calm—she's just trying to provoke you. Don't give her the satisfaction.* "Will this be all for you today?"

"For now. Ty and I are trying to work things out. I mean—we *are* still married, for heaven's sake", she shared as she tossed her blonde hair behind her shoulders.

Kendall's hands froze in the register drawer as Cameron's words sunk in. *"Still married?"*

"Yeah—didn't he tell you yet? Our divorce was never finalized. And since we a*re* married, we decided to give us another shot—"

"Oh—"

"—So if all goes well tonight, I'll be back for another box of these in a couple days."

Somehow Kendall managed to count change and then handed it to Cameron with trembling hands.

"Have a good evening, Miss Porter. I know *I* will", she called over her shoulder as she departed.

Ty and Cameron were still married?

No wonder he hasn't called. Ty's been… busy.

Kendall could barely suppress the anger that boiled inside her. Her chest felt tight, swamped with heartache.

Ty and Cameron were still married…

"Are you alright?" Marcus, her pharmacy assistant, questioned.

"I-I'm fine."

"Honey, you're paler than a Speedo-wearing European on his first Florida vacation! It's slow tonight. Why don't you go on home? I can finish up the next two hours by myself."

"You're sure?—you don't mind closing up alone?"

"Absolutely sure."

The debacle back at the pharmacy replayed in Kendall's mind during the short ride home. Somehow she managed to curb the anger and agony. But as soon as she was safely tucked behind the walls of her cozy Craftsman bungalow, the anguish consumed her. Drifting toward the sofa, she collapsed—crying— allowing the despair to ripple through her.

Ty was still married...

God, how could she have been so stupid?— careless?—naïve?

She had allowed herself to fall in love with a married man...

No wonder he wanted a casual relationship. He'd probably known from the very beginning the odds were good that Cameron would return one day (and had even concocted a way to ensure his physiological needs were met until that day came). Kendall had been so blinded by the attention that her long-time crush had given her, she'd happily obliged.

Your intuition has never steered you wrong. You were warned. You just chose to ignore it.

Yes, she had ignored it. Alarms *had* sounded. What she wouldn't give to go back and do things differently.

Chapter 19

Randall was seeing things—*had to be hallu-cinating*! He'd been standing in the firehouse kitchen, talking to Jimmy about purchasing and restoring Mr. Morgan's old 1983 Boston Whaler, when a woman with an uncanny resemblance to Cameron Everitt barged in.

"Good evening, boys. Is Ty around?"

"In his office", Jimmy disclosed.

"Thanks."

They watched as Cameron sashayed down the hall to Ty's office. Jimmy waited until the door closed behind her before turning his attention back to Randall. "What the hell is *she* doin' here?"

Randall leaned his backside against the counter, crossing his arms over his chest as he stared in disbelief down the hall toward Ty's office. "Beats me."

He and Jimmy remained in the kitchen until the clock struck seven, signaling the end to their shift and the beginning of on-call duty. The door to Lieutenant Everitt's office was still closed as he threw his duffle bag over his shoulder. He couldn't hear

anything—either they were having a civil conversation or they were using their mouths for... *other
purposes.*

Pushing the heavy metal door that led to the bay
garage open, Randall pointed his work boots toward
his truck. The full moon illuminated the small parking
lot as he stepped into the breezy night, ironically
shedding light on what he knew he had to do.

"You up for a pitcher of beer and a few rounds of
pool?" Jimmy asked as he tossed his bag into the bed of
his truck. "There's a city commission meeting tonight.
Lana won't be home for at least another hour and a
half."

Tempting—*very tempting*—but he had somewhere he needed to be. "Maybe some other time." He
had to break the news to Kendall. Cameron was back
and he knew his best friend—the woman he was in
love with—needed a shoulder to lean on.

And, damn it, that person was going to be him.

After leaving the fire station, Randall detoured
to Kendall's house. Her car was parked in the drive.
Good. She was home. Because this wasn't the type of
conversation he necessarily wanted to have in public.

Maneuvering his large truck into the driveway,
he parked, and then made his way toward the front
porch. Knowing already that the front door was locked,
he shifted the doormat, revealing the key she kept
hidden underneath. Inserting the key, he gave it a
twist, making sure to restore it to its rightful location
once the door was unlocked.

"Kendall", he called out as he opened the door,
"you in here? You know, you really need to find a new
hiding spot for your spare key. Anyone could just walk

in here and—"

And that's when he saw her.

Kendall. Lying on the couch, clinging to a throw pillow, mascara losing the battle against gravity as a steady stream of black tears fled her gorgeous amber eyes.

"Shit, Babe", Randall mumbled as he moved toward her. Sighing, he took a seat on the couch next to her. "Come here."

Kendall flung herself into Randall's open arms, resting her head on his shoulder. She hated crying—especially over a man—but sometimes desperate times called for desperate measures. "R-rand?"

"Yes?"

"C-can you do me a favor?"

Randall closed his eyes, caressing the back of her head in an attempt to comfort her. "Anything, Babe."

"Please don't t-tell me 'I told you s-so.' "

Randall held her a little tighter, letting her tears saturate his navy fire department T-shirt. He wasn't certain how long they remained in the embrace—*long enough for his right shoulder to become completely soaked.* It felt good to hold her again, although he despised the reason why it was necessary. Men didn't take pleasure in witnessing tears—at least no man that he knew of. Especially when said tears were shed by the women they loved.

Lifting her head, Kendall swiped at her face. "I'm sure you've h-heard by now, huh?"

"Cameron's back", he said as he swept a strand of hair away from her left eye.

Kendall nodded. "And... apparently she and Ty are still married."

"Wait—*what?*"

"Cameron came by the pharmacy earlier. She bought a box of condoms and gloated about their marital status. According to her, they're toying with the idea of getting back together."

"Shit..." Randall scrubbed his hand down his face and sighed. "She came by the station tonight."

"She did?"

He nodded. "About half an hour before my shift ended. She went into his office and shut the door... When I left they were still in there."

Kendall drew in a shaky breath and slowly exhaled. Right now—at this very moment—Ty likely had Cameron pinned against the fire truck, engaging in make-up sex... "Guess you were right, Rand: men do 'casual' much better than women. I'm not cut out for this"—she uttered as she gestured toward her mascara-streaked face—"obviously. I'm sorry. Gosh, I'm such a mess!"

He watched as Kendall swiped at her face again with her fingertips, erasing the dark vertical lines from her cheeks. Funny how she thought she looked a mess; he thought she looked beautiful. "You look gorgeous, Kendall. You *always* look gorgeous..."

Kendall looked into his eyes and smiled. "You wanna stay for dinner? I really don't want to be alone right now."

Seeing her smile was well worth the gallon of tears she'd shed on his shoulder moments earlier. "Of course, I'll stay."

The steady thump of the rubber ball bouncing off the wall in Ty's office echoed in the empty fire-house. The pattern was soothing. Throw. Bounce. Catch. Throw. Bounce. Catch. His feet lay crossed on top of his desk, his back comfortably pressed against the fake leather that lined the back of the chair. He did some of his best thinking like this...

Cameron had just left moments ago. She'd waltzed in here with wicked intentions, attempting to use her body to persuade him into giving their marriage another go-around.

It hadn't worked.

After he kindly asked her to put her clothes back on, they had a surprisingly pleasant chat. "Surprising" because typically when Cam didn't get her way, she became... difficult (which explains the sports car he'd purchased and the second mortgage he'd taken out to fund the pool and remodel a few years ago).

Maybe she was finally growing up—*or maybe she realized she no longer had you by the balls.*

He'd made his wishes clear: he wanted out of the marriage. No more games. She agreed to file the paperwork by the end of the week and then planted a farewell kiss on his cheek.

As soon as he was alone, he reached for his phone and called Kendall. She didn't answer—he hadn't expected her to. Although that didn't stop him from calling again. He lost track of how many messages he'd left. If he had to make a guess, he'd estimate somewhere around a dozen.

Throw. Bounce. Catch.

Clearly she had no intention of speaking to him tonight. Odds were good she'd already stumbled upon the news that he was still legally married (this was Butler Island, after all—juicy gossip like this was just too good to keep quiet for long).

Throw. Bounce. Catch. Throw. Bounce. Catch.

She was avoiding his calls—that much was obvious. But it was hard to ignore someone when they were standing directly in front of you... Placing the rubber ball on his desk, he grabbed the dispatch radio and snagged the keys to the paramedic truck. He'd stand on her front porch all night if that's what it took for her to talk to him.

Ty took a right out of the station, heading west until he came upon Third Street. It didn't take long to realize that Kendall had company: Randall's black F-150 was parked in the drive behind her Maxima. Ty slowed and then halted in front of the pale yellow bungalow he'd spent countless nights in: eating dinner, laughing, loving.

He'd gone about this all wrong. Should've driven his ass over here the moment he'd left Bayside Cottages two days ago. Kendall was entitled to an explanation—deserved to hear it from his mouth. But it looked as though that wasn't going to happen tonight.

Tonight she had company...

Just then, an eerie sensation crept up his spine, raising the hair on the back of his neck. Was it customary for Kendall to have *company* the nights he was on shift?

Okay, the more he thought about it, the more absurd it seemed.

She's nothing like Cam. There isn't a devious bone in her flawless body.

Kendall didn't have to resort to trickery or deceitful ploys for people to fall in love with her.

He glanced at Randall's truck in the drive one last time before pressing his foot on the gas. Evidently Ty wasn't the only man fond of the town's only pharmacist. After turning around in the cul-de-sac, he ventured back to the firehouse. Tomorrow he was going to make it his mission to speak to her. She deserved an explanation.

Ty just prayed he wasn't too late.

Chapter 20

The following morning proved to be a difficult one: Kendall was heavy with regret and nearly crippled with nausea. Forging ahead, she managed to get dressed and strolled into Porter Pharmacy with minutes to spare, relieved to find that Marcus had arrived to open the store alongside her.

He shared his concern, affirming that she appeared worse than she had the evening before—even suggesting she return home to rest—but Kendall had kindly dismissed his offer, recognizing that the distraction work provided was exactly what she needed today.

After prepping for the day ahead, Kendall unlocked the glass door and flipped the hanging sign, signaling to customers that the pharmacy was open. She promptly returned to the back counter, ready to begin analyzing the list of prescriptions scheduled to be picked up later today, when Debbie Handler (also known as "Chatty Debbie") appeared before her with a package of throat lozenges.

"Good mornin', Kendall. How are you?"

"Hi, Mrs. Handler. I'm doing well—and you?"

Debbie tugged on her glasses until they were perched on the tip of her nose and leaned forward for a closer inspection. "You sure 'bout that?—you don't look so good this morning. That pretty face of yours looks to be about ten shades of green!"

So much for the thin layer of bronzer you pain-stakingly applied this morning. "There's been a nasty stomach virus circulating through the elementary this week. I guess it's *possible* I could be coming down with it, too—we've seen an influx of parents and infected children this week searching for various items to sooth their symptoms."

Mrs. Handler pushed her glasses back into po-sition and reached behind her for a bottle of hand sanitizer. "Guess I'd better add this to my purchase today, too", she said as she placed the container on the counter next to the package of throat lozenges. "One can never be too careful!"

"That's true", Kendall agreed as she scanned the two items.

"I have a pretty strong immune system—haven't been sick in years. And it's a good thing, too"—Debbie cupped her hand around her mouth and lowered her voice for emphasis—"because I have a tendency to projectile-vomit…"

Oh, no—here we go!

"…I'm told it's due to having strong abdominal muscles, but I'd like to think it has more to do with my ability to detect unpleasantries. When I was pregnant with Kelly forty years ago, the smell of a grocery store nearly brought me to my knees. After three separate vomiting incidents in aisle two, the owner of the store at the time, Mr. Paul, banned me from the store…"

Pregnancy? Kendall's queasy stomach was the

result of a crushing heartache and a potential viral infection. Wasn't it?

"… it was awful!—I had to waddle around the store with a clothes pin clamped around my nose! And let me tell ya, breathing through your mouth for an hour while nine months pregnant is no easy feat!"

Kendall smiled nervously as she bagged Chatty Debbie's purchases and handed her the change. "I'm sure it wasn't."

"You take care, honey", Mrs. Handler called out as she headed toward the exit.

Once she was alone, Kendall ransacked her brain, trying to recall the date of her last period. Could she be pregnant?

There was only one way to find out.

Kendall strolled down aisle four until she came upon the shelf that housed the pharmacy's selection of pregnancy tests. She snatched a random box from the display, tucking it beneath her arm incase Marcus or an unsuspecting customer put two and two together.

Thinking back to the colored birth-control pills she swallowed every morning, she realized she *was* late—roughly two weeks late. It wasn't something she'd been too worried about; this wasn't the first time stress had affected her menstrual cycle.

And let's face it: the last several weeks had been a rollercoaster of highs and lows.

The odds of her being pregnant were about as likely as winning the state lottery. Slim. Very slim. But the negative results would give her peace of mind. And when the smothering heartache eased and the viral infection ran its course, she'd once again join the mass of women enslaved to Tampax until their ovaries withered into useless, dormant organs.

Retreating into the employee bathroom in the rear of the store, Kendall opened the box and followed the manufacturer's instructions, holding the plastic stick under her urine stream for several moments until the tip was saturated. She then placed the stick on the edge of the sink, lowered her black pencil skirt into its rightful position, and paced the small restroom for what seemed like the longest three minutes of her life.

Convinced that enough time had passed, she cautiously stepped toward the sink and glanced at the tiny display. Her heart took a nosedive toward her toes as the image sunk in: two pink lines.

"Oh, no", she whispered, briefly closing her eyes.

See what happens when you spend hours crying, forgetting to remove your contacts, and only managing to steal an hour or two of sleep?—you hallucinate!

Kendall willed her eyes to open, scanning the small display window once again. One line was dark, one was faint.

Probably a faulty test.

Yeah, that had to be it. Because she *couldn't* be pregnant. But then again, how many times had she counseled disbelieving female customers that'd encountered... similar circumstances. Plenty.

And what had she always told them? *Unfortunately it doesn't matter if one line appears darker than the other. If you see two lines, you're positively pregnant.*

In fact, it was only roughly three months ago she'd had this discussion with Carla Reddington. She'd taken six, accusing Kendall of stocking the pharmacy with faulty tests. Of course, she later apologized, blaming her incoherency on raging hormones. But that's where the similarities ended (Carla was happily married—Kendall was impregnated with a married man's child).

Obviously karma was none too happy that she'd been sleeping with a married man—didn't matter that she hadn't known it at the time.

She was a mistress, carrying her lover's child, while he was probably in the sack with his wife at this very moment, putting the condoms Cameron purchased yesterday to good use. In fact, they were probably having a good laugh at her expense. Kendall allowed herself to believe the night she'd spent in Ty's bed had been the turning point in their relationship. Like it was the beginning of something strong, solid.

Real.

What a fool she'd been.

Pulling herself together, she washed her hands, carefully disguising the test in a brown paper towel, when an unmistakable sensation washed over her.

Sudden onset of sweat. Quivering hands. Weakness.

Kendall barely made it back to the porcelain throne before the contents of her bagel and last night's dinner defied the laws of gravity.

She'd really made a mess of her life. Some particularly tough decisions would have to be made.

And soon.

"Where've you been?" he asked as he lowered the newspaper.

"I took a drive."

"I thought we agreed you needed to lie low for a while."

"That's what I've been doing—but a person can only stand to look at four walls for so long before they—"

Closing the newspaper, he stood and stalked toward his accomplice. "We had a deal: I conduct surveillance, while you stay hidden."

"I really don't see the big deal. I was careful. And besides, you'd be doing the same thing if the shoe were on the other foot."

"Wrong. I would've never been in your shoes in the first place. Because—unlike you—I have impulse control. Your stupid little spray-painting stunt a few weeks ago could've cost us this job! In fact, why don't we just pack up and leave?—find another target?" His accomplice's eyes widened.

"No. No, you were right. The payoff from this job will be well worth the wait—even if the wait includes me remaining in this room until showtime..." The accomplice was growing impatient (and really tired of taking orders). They were supposed to be "partners"—not master and slave!

Keep your eye on the prize. Soon you'll have everything you've ever wanted.

Sucking in a hefty liter of air, the accomplice silently agreed to lie and wait. Because in a matter of weeks—maybe even days—they'd pay Porter Pharmacy another visit. And what a disastrous occurrence it would be...

Chapter 21

"What do you mean *she left?*" Ty asked as he braced his hands on the edge of the pharmacy counter.

"She wasn't feeling well—truthfully, she probably should've just stayed home in bed! But you know Kendall: her work ethic teeters on the edge of being a bit obsessive—it's in her genes."

"About how long ago did she leave?"

Marcus looked over his shoulder at the clock hanging on the wall and shrugged. "I don't know, thirty—maybe forty-five—minutes ago."

"Thanks", Ty uttered, pushing away from the counter.

"Oh—but I wouldn't head over there, if I were you."

"Why not?"

"She doesn't have a nagging cough or a simple headache." Marcus cupped his hands around his mouth and leaned across the counter, making sure to speak in a loud whisper. "It's the stomach flu…"

"Okaaay", he drew out, not quite understanding the point Kendall's assistant was trying to make.

"She's real pale and... *she isn't a quiet vomiter.*"

Evidently, Marcus did not have a strong stomach. Guess it was a good thing Ty did. "I'm a firefighter/paramedic, Marcus. Trust me, I've handled far worse."

After his conversation with Marcus, Ty climbed into his truck and drove to Kendall's, relying on repetition to get him there. Funny how his truck automatically knew where to go—he'd been deep in thought during the three minute drive. Next thing he knew, he was idling in her driveway. It was almost as if his white Ford F-250 had a mind of its own.

Good. Glad one of them was thinking clearly.

Taking in a hefty gulp of air, Ty wandered toward the front porch, knocked on the front door several times, then waited. And waited.

No answer.

Growing worried, he shifted the mat to reveal the spare key and then proceeded to unlock the door. He was immediately assaulted with her scent: orange blossoms. He'd missed it. The floral essence had lingered on his pillow that first night, but by the next morning it was gone.

"Kendall!" he called out after closing the door. He entered cautiously, ready to take the stairs two at a time to her loft bedroom, when he heard a faint noise coming from the downstairs guest bathroom. Trekking down the narrow hall, the unmistakable sound of retching swelled with intensity.

Ty softly knocked on the door. "Kendall, are you okay?"

There was a sequence of coughs and then a weak, "What do you wa—*oh, no—not again!*"

It sounded as though she were upchucking a meal from last week—the near-deafening tenor echoing against the tile with powerful precision. Marcus was right: Kendall wasn't a quiet vomiter. Reaching into the linen closet, he snagged a washcloth and headed to the kitchen. He placed the rag under the faucet—making sure to wring out the excess—filled a small cup with water, and then retraced his steps back to the bathroom.

"I'm coming in", he announced as he nudged the door open. And, damn, if his heart didn't break at the sight of her: on her knees in a tight black skirt, one shoe missing, her cardigan haphazardly tossed on the floor beside her, leaving her in a thin lacy top.

Kneeling beside her, he placed the cold wet rag on the back of her neck. "Water?"

Kendall settled back onto her heels, nodding as she reached for the glass with trembling hands. She swallowed a few sips and then closed her eyes. "You should go. Before you get sick", she managed feebly.

Ty swept a strand of hair away from her eye. "Think I'll take my chances."

His fingers brushed against her cheek, forcing her eyes to suddenly open. He couldn't believe how pale she was—how her normally vibrant amber eyes were sunken and red. And the most unbelievable part?

She *still* looked beautiful—even at her worst.

"I'm fine—*really*."

"You don't look it. Here", he gestured toward the cup, "take another drink."

Kendall swallowed more water—not because he told her to—but because she was incredibly thirsty. "What're you doing here?"

"Marcus said you went home sick. I wanted to stop by and check on you."

"And I'm fine now. So you can go."

Ty wiped his hand down his face in frustration—something he seemed to be experiencing a lot these days—and glanced at the pedestal sink. Specifically the two plastic sticks lying on the edge. "Stomach flu?" he asked as he stood up for a closer inspection.

"Uh, yeah. Something like that..."

With Kendall's back still turned, Ty carefully picked up one of the sticks, confirming his suspicions. Now, he was no pregnancy test expert, but two pink lines, coupled with the image of Kendall hugging the commode, could only mean one thing: she was pregnant. "Sort of like a nine-month virus?"

Her eyes quickly cut to Ty, holding one of the tests. Yes, she'd taken two more at home—both positive—and had completely forgotten about them lying openly on the edge of the sink.

"You're pregnant", he stated.

"Apparently."

"And when were you planning to tell me?—huh?"

Kendall managed to conjure up the strength to get back on her feet. "I don't know, Ty—when were you planning to mention that you're *still* married?"

Closing his eyes briefly, he whispered, "You heard."

"Sure did—Cameron couldn't wait to share that bit of information. She stopped in the pharmacy yesterday for a news flash and a box of condoms." Brushing past him, she started down the hall.

"I didn't sleep with her", he conceded as he followed behind.

Kendall wobbled into the kitchen, still only wearing one shoe. "She's your wife. Your sex-life is none of my business—at least, not anymore."

"Listen, I can explain. She—"

"Not interested", she uttered weakly as she opened the pantry door. Balancing on the balls of her feet, she stretched overhead for the box of saltine crackers positioned on the top shelf, but they were just out of reach.

Refusing to standby while she struggled, Ty snatched the box and handed it to her. "I didn't know I was still married. I signed the papers—I swear to you, I did. I never would've pursued a relationship with you if I'd have known about this."

"So you're saying she tricked you?" Her words came out sounding more like a disbelieving statement than a question.

"Yeah, that about sums it up. Apparently she thought revealing the truth would suddenly make everything go back to how it was before."

"And when she visited you at the station last night with a newly-purchased box of condoms?—"

"I told her I wasn't interested; I wanted out. Immediately."

With her free hand, she covered her eyes and sighed. "This is insane…"

"I know it is. But that's how Cameron operates— she has a twisted mind." Ty gestured toward the package of crackers still clutched in her hand. "Eat."

Kendall reached into the package with trembling hands and took a small bite, wincing as she slowly chewed.

"What's wrong?"

"My mouth's so dry."

Stepping around her, he moved toward the fridge and tugged on the handle. "Looks like somebody went grocery shopping recently", he uttered as he snatched a can of ginger ale from the top shelf. Ty popped the tab of the aluminum can and handed it to her. "Here, sip this. It'll help settle your stomach."

He observed as she slowly took in the fizzy liquid. *Kendall was pregnant...* Raising the plastic stick still in his grasp, he asked, "When did you find out?"

Setting the can of ginger ale on the counter, Kendall wrapped her arms around her middle for comfort. "About two hours ago. I wasn't feeling well last night, but I didn't take the test until this morning."

Ty thought back to last night—the part where he'd driven by and found Randall's truck in the drive, in particular. He scratched the back of his head and sighed. She was probably going to be offended, but he had to know. "I have to ask... Is it mine?"

"*Excuse me?*" she asked incredulously.

"The baby—is it—?"

"What kind of question is that?"

"Um, the same question any man in my position might ask." Eyes like daggers, she stared at him.

Okay, he sort of expected that reaction. But he needed to be sure. And now that he was, he needed to explain where the small amount of lingering doubt had come from. "I drove by last night—after Cam left the station. I wanted to talk to you—see you. But Randall's truck was parked in the driveway and... and it sort of got me thinking."

"Thinking what, exactly?"

"About what you do the nights I'm on shift."

Was he serious? "I haven't slept with anyone but you in months, Ty", she stated firmly. Why was he suddenly giving *her* the third degree?

"I thought you said you were on the pill."

"I am."

Ty shoved the heels of his hands against his closed lids and applied gentle pressure. "So how did this happen, huh? Did you plan this the night you surprised me at the fire station?"

Kendall pushed away from the counter and stepped toward him, still only wearing one shoe. "How. Dare. You. I may be a lot of things, Ty. But I'm not a conniving, manipulative twit like your ex—oh, excuse me—*current*—wife."

She was right. Kendall was nothing like his ex—*current*—wife. Purposely getting pregnant was just the kind of deceitful scheme Cam would've employed. Suddenly feeling a bit better about his newly-discovered fatherhood status, he asked the next logical question. "So, what're we gonna do?"

"We?—*we* aren't going to do anything. I can take care of myself."

"You're not doing this alone', he reprimanded. Sighing, he wiped his palm down his face again in an attempt to simmer his growing temper. "My divorce should be finalized in a few weeks. When that happens, we'll go down to the county courthouse and get married. You can move in with me and—"

Kendall shook her head. "No", she stated candidly. "I'm not marrying you. And I'm *not* moving in with you."

"C'mon, Doll, check your ego at the door."

"*My Ego*? If anyone's on an ego trip—it's *you*! Marching in here, acting like an arrogant, narcissistic... macho... bastard. In fact, why don't you just clobber me over the head and drag me back to your cave by the hair!"

"I'm going to overlook your poor attempt at describing my personality traits because I think we both know, you know me better than that... I'm trying to do the right thing here", he amended.

And that was part of the problem. He didn't want to marry her because he *loved* her; he wanted to marry her because he felt obligated. She didn't want that. Couldn't bear to wake up next to him every morning knowing she was only there because of the baby. "I'm leaving", she blurted.

"What do you mean your?—"

"I took the job in Jacksonville", she admitted softly.

"Wait—when did you decide that?"

"Yesterday."

"You can't leave! You're pregnant with my—"

"It's a done deal." *Mostly.*

Ty glared. She may not have deliberately gotten pregnant, but she was consciously eliminating his role as father. "Not a conniving, manipulative twit, huh? Could've fooled me."

"Get. Out", she punctuated through clenched teeth. And when he didn't budge, she allowed the anger that'd bubbled just below the surface to erupt. "I said, get out!"

Ty pushed away from the counter and headed toward the front door with an agile, angry gait. As soon as the door slammed behind him, he regretted his animosity. He'd purposely baited her—all because his marriage proposal had been rejected.

Marriage proposal?—you call that a marriage proposal?

Okay, come to think of it, it had sounded rather impersonal. Trivial.

Pausing on the bottom porch step, he toyed with the idea of going back inside—confessing that baby or no baby, he was in love with her. That the news of her leaving had felt like a swift kick to the chest.

But she was too angry—too hurt—to hear that right now. She needed time to calm down. And he needed time to figure out how he was going to convince Kendall that his marriage proposal had nothing to do with the baby and everything to do with how much he loved her.

Ty jumped into his truck and looked at the positive pregnancy test still clutched in his hand. *He was going to be a father...*

Somehow he was going to fix this. He'd been a single parent before—when he'd taken Olivia in after their parents' fatal accident nearly nineteen years ago—and by no means was it a glamorous job. No way was he going to stand by and allow Kendall to take on that responsibility by herself.

No way was he going to give up on his new family.

Chapter 22

"Mom?—Dad?—you in here?" Kendall shouted as she shut the screen door behind her. Immediately she was accosted with the aroma of her childhood: a nostalgic blend of potpourri, remnants of her mother's Aqua Net hairspray, and the scent of a delicious home-cooked meal.

"Out here on the deck, dear!" her mother called out.

Kendall meandered through the living room, weaving through the mass of statues and knick-knacks randomly displayed around the room. She fought the urge to move the hideous-looking sculpture of a Basset Hound, staring with its eyes crossed at a butterfly that'd landed on the tip of its nose. Her mother was quick to notice when one of her possessions had been tampered with, something she and her father took pleasure in doing when she was younger. In fact, they'd even place bets on how long it'd take before her mother would carefully nudge the decoration back into its rightful position.

Kendall and her father would look at one

another and laugh while her mother would tap her
toes on the wood floor, placing her hands on her hips.
Alright, you two—which one of you did it? She would
say.

Don't know what you're talkin' about, Ellen. Her
father would declare. Gosh, she missed hearing his
voice. Missed the conversations they used to have
and his contagious belly laugh—the kind that made
his shoulders shake up and down. She was so
grateful that he survived the stroke, but she hated to
see him bound to a wheelchair, only communicating
by blinking his left eye: once for no, twice for yes.

Kendall slid the screen door that led to the deck
open, hugging her parents before taking a seat at the
picnic table.

"You're just in time for dinner", her mother
said. "I made lasagna. Help yourself."

"Thanks, but I'm not that hungry."

"You?—not hungry? What's goin' on, dear? You
never pass on my lasagna."

"I'm okay, mom." *At least, I hope I will be.* "Actually, I already ate." *A half package of Saltine Crackers—
salt-side down. Geez, she was becoming more particular
and ridiculous by the day.* "I, uh… have something I
need to talk to the two of you about."

"We're all ears, dear", her mother assured her.

Okay, so she should probably begin by men-
tioning she was… expecting. But the fact that she was
unwed and the father was *still* married was likely too
much shock for one evening. So instead, she decided to
share her recent career decision. "I was offered a position at a large-chain pharmacy in Jacksonville. And…
I'm going to take it. I'll hire a qualified replacement to
manage the day-to-day tasks here. And I'll still remain owner—still make all the crucial decisions."

Kendall waited for the backlash. Anticipating the moment when her mother's cool façade would crack. But surprisingly that didn't happen. Instead, her mother gently placed her fork on the plate, wiped the corners of her mouth with her paper napkin, and smiled.

Feeding off the positive energy, Kendall covered her father's frail hands with her palms, and spoke directly to him. "I know Porter Pharmacy was your creation and you always wanted me to carry on your legacy... but..."

"Honey", her mother cut in, "you have to do what makes *you* happy. We always knew there'd come a day you'd want to pack up and move on. Frankly, we thought this day would've come much sooner."

Kendall gave her father's hands a squeeze and looked into his eyes. "So you're okay with this?" she whispered.

Her father blinked twice: *yes.*

Days later, Kendall slid into the corner booth at the local diner where Olivia awaited. She plucked the menu from the metal holder, scanning the grease-stained paper with utter fascination. "Gosh, I'm starving!" she shared.

"Well, you're eatin' for two, now."

Aside from Ty, Olivia and Grant were the only people that knew about her... *condition.* She hadn't yet assembled the courage to tell Randall. He'd act happy for her—no doubt—but deep down, she knew he'd be crushed. Kendall added the dreaded conversation to her lengthy to-do list. It had to happen soon. Because the last thing she wanted was for Rand to hear about it from someone else. That would just be downright tacky.

"I did inventory today—worked right through lunch!"

"Kendall! You shouldn't be skippin' meals, ya know", Olivia reprimanded.

"Oh, don't worry; I'm going to make up for it!" When the waitress came over, Kendall ordered her usual: a juicy double bacon cheeseburger with a side of crispy onion rings.

"So things are busy at the pharmacy?"

Kendall nodded. "Since I'll be transitioning to part-time in two weeks, there's a lot of loose ends to tie up. Not to mention, I have several interviews scheduled for my replacement."

Olivia supported her chin with her hand and studied Kendall from across the table.

"What?" Kendall finally asked.

Shrugging, Olivia answered, "Nothing. It's just... I can't believe you're actually goin' through with this."

Kendall swirled her sweet tea with her straw. "It's what I've always wanted. And besides, there's nothing here for me."

"That's not true and you know it! You have me, your parents, Randall... *and Ty.*"

"Liv", she warned.

"What? I'm just pointin' out that you have people in this town that really love you."

Kendall coughed, nearly choking on her sweet tea. "Ty doesn't fit into that category—"

"You sure 'bout that? The man has been a complete grouch—so I've been told—and he's already begun baby proofing his house, for Heaven's sake!"

"Roughly forty-five percent of all unintentional injury deaths in children occur in and around the home", Kendall recited flatly.

"Do you hear yourself?"

"Okay", she conceded, "he cares—about the ba-by—"

"And you."

Kendall shook her head. "I don't want to talk about this anymore. Tell me about your honeymoon."

Olivia beamed with happiness. 'Well, I'd love to tell you how soft the sand felt under my toes, or how incredibly clear the water looked. But... we sort of didn't get out. Much."

Kendall laughed (something she hadn't done in a long time). "So the *glow* you're wearing has nothing to do with the Caribbean sun?"

"Nope, it's the kind of glow that can only come from within!"

"Well, it looks good on you", Kendall shared before taking a sip of her tea.

"It looked really good on you, too—the night of my weddin'." Olivia observed as her best friend stared longingly into her sweet tea, as if remembering that night, then fidgeted about when she recalled the chaos that ensued the following morning. "Don't think I didn't notice that the best man and the maid of honor went *missin'* after sharin' a slow dance by the bonfire." The pain was clearly written all over Kendall's face. "What's *really* goin' on with you two, Kendall? I mean, you can't honestly believe that he still has feelings for his sorry-excuse-of-an-ex-wife."

Saved by the gum-chewing, lip-smacking wait-ress, Kendall salivated at the sight of her dinner. Unable to resist, she popped a steaming-hot onion ring into her mouth and moaned in delight. "Mmm, that's *so good*! I just may have to place a to-go order of onion rings to munch on later this evening during *Grey's Anatomy*."

Olivia smothered her salad in Italian dressing and then sat the empty plastic container on the table. "I'm waitin'..."

Sighing, Kendall finally caved. "I really don't know what to say. We were... *together*. And now we're not."

"Have you spoken to him?"

Kendall shook her head while she finished chewing. "There's not much to say."

"You're carrying his child—my niece or nephew—in there", Olivia reminded her as she gestured toward Kendall's belly.

"Shhh!"

"Sorry", Olivia whispered. "Don't you think the two of you should bury the hatchet? I mean, whether you like it or not, Ty is goin' to be a part of your life. Forever."

"I know that. And I'm not some deceitful broad, plotting to use his baby against him as punishment. I would *never* keep him from his child. Ever. But neither will I stick around this nosy town for the sake of making *his* life easier."

"So that's it—you're leavin'."

Kendall took another sip of her sweet tea and shrugged. "It's a four hour drive, Liv. We'll figure out all the details of visitations at some point. I mean, we have until November before the baby's due."

They ate in silence for some time (which Kendall was thankful for). There was nothing worse than discussing something serious over a meal—it tended to make your mind focus on everything but how delectable every bite tasted. In fact, if she knew she'd be engaging in an important discussion, she'd rather eat something like... alfalfa sprouts. That way, she could speak her mind and almost forget she was eating grass.

"When's your first day?" Olivia finally asked. She didn't have to like that her best friend was skipping town, but she was still determined to be supportive.

"May first."

"Do they know your preg—know about you *medical condition?*" she amended.

Kendall smiled and nodded. "I spoke to the manager last week—in case he wanted to hire someone else. But he assured me it wouldn't be an issue."

Popping another onion ring into her mouth, she thought about the night Ty had forged his way into her home, clutching her favorite meal in a grease-stained bag. It seemed everything in this town—even onion rings—reminded her of Ty. And the sooner she left Butler Island, the sooner the painful memories would fade.

At least she hoped they would.

Chapter 23

It didn't take much for the residents of Butler Island to come up with a reason to throw a shindig on the beach. And when news spread that the city's beloved pharmacist was skipping town, a going away party was practically inevitable.

Billows of smoke scaled the flames as the large pile of wood burned, keeping the mosquitoes at bay and the ambiance casual and light-hearted. There wasn't a cloud in the sky and the steady breeze still carried a hint of spring chill.

Ty stood in the background, quietly observing as residents offered Kendall farewells and good fortune. He hadn't spoken to her since the morning he discovered he was going to be a father. He'd always thought he didn't want children—he'd spent the better part of his adult life raising Olivia. Of course, he wouldn't have had it any other way. But the idea of starting over—raising another child—had always terrified him (or maybe subconsciously, the thought of having a child with Cameron had had him twisted with fear).

And now the only thing that scared Ty: living four hours from his child and the woman he loved.

He was going to make it his mission to speak to her tonight.

Ty kept an eye on the raven-haired beauty while he mingled with the crowd, searching for the perfect opportunity to make his move. Seemed she'd spoken to everyone tonight—everyone except him. But that was about to change.

"I still can't believe you're really leaving. It's been a pleasure working with you", Marcus confessed.

Kendall stepped forward and wrapped her arms around his small frame. "Thank you, Marcus, although you're not entirely rid of me yet. I still haven't found a replacement."

"Well, I hope you won't be offended when I say: *I hope it takes a while.*"

Chuckling softly, she replied, "No, not at all." Kendall allowed her eyes to briefly scan over the crowd. She still couldn't believe the amount of people that'd come to wish her well. She was truly touched. But having spent the last hour and a half assuring everyone that (a) Porter Pharmacy would remain open, (b) her father wasn't upset, and (c) she would remain in Butler Island at least until a qualified replacement could be located, had exhausted her rather quickly.

"Excuse me, will you?" Slipping away from Marcus and the remainder of the crowd, Kendall shuffled her bare feet through the powdery sand until she came upon the water's edge. The moon's reflection skidded across the calm Gulf of Mexico, its splendor soothing her rattled nerves.

She inhaled a deep breath of salty air. One of the many benefits of living in Florida: one was only about an hour's drive from the nearest beach—at most. Jacksonville was nestled along the Atlantic Coast— the beach roughly ten minutes from her new job. She planned to visit often once she became a permanent resident of the largest city in the Sunshine State. She wondered if it smelled the same... As if doubting the salt to water ratio between the massive Atlantic Ocean and the Gulf of Mexico, she filled her lungs to maximum capacity, memorizing the wistful aroma.

"This feels a little bit like déjà vu", Ty uttered as he approached from behind.

Kendall smiled. "Lucky for me, I didn't spill my drink this time."

Ty laughed, recalling how she'd spilled her entire beer down the front of her shirt on New Year's Eve. "Pretty good turn out tonight, huh?"

"Yeah", she admitted on a sigh. "I honestly didn't expect everyone in town to make such a fuss."

Ty shoved both hands into his front pockets up to his knuckles and focused his gaze on the horizon. "Well, that's because everybody loves you, Kendall."

Everyone but you... "Well, I wouldn't go *that* far, but... thanks."

The sound of waves lapping against the shore enveloped them for some time. There was so much he wanted to know—so much he wanted to say—but he questioned whether the timing was right. "So when's your first day in Jacksonville?" he decided to start with.

"Monday."

Ty nodded, making sure to choose his next question carefully. It'd been almost three weeks since they'd spoken and the last thing he wanted to do was argue. "Find a replacement yet?"

"Still looking. I have two interviews set up for later next week, though."

Damn it, this was *killing* him! Why couldn't he just tell her how he felt?—that he was deliriously and completely in love with her? *Because your admission still wouldn't make her stay...*

"*Kendall, come here*", Vicki and Lana called out in unison. "*You have to see this!*"

Her gaze averted from her friends at the bonfire to the man standing beside her. Their eyes met and held for a few long beats. And if she didn't know better, she'd have sworn he was about to tell her something important, but in an instant his solemn expression turned neutral.

Ty tipped his head toward the bonfire. "Go on, Doll. We'll talk later." She nodded once and then retreated back to the celebration. In two days, she'd be starting a new chapter in her life. What he wouldn't give to be a part of it.

"I'm telling you, this is the perfect time to strike. She's working part-time now, which means she's most likely distracted."

"I don't know. I still haven't been able to figure out what—if any—security measures were implemented inside. A buddy of mine in Panama City Beach is looking into it for me."

"No need. I figured out how we can get in and out without the risk of tripping the alarm."

The large man in charge crossed his arms over his broad chest. "Alright, I'm listening..."

"I know where Kendall Porter lives—and better

yet—I happen to know that she always keeps the spare key to her front door hidden beneath the welcome mat."

"How's that going to help us get the goods at the pharmacy without sounding the alarm?"

The small accomplice smiled deviously. "Because Kendall Porter will be accompanying us." The shorter of the two went on to divulge the specifics of the proposed plan, making sure to counter every *what if* with a solid response. Maybe the many hours spent in seclusion really had paid off.

"I don't know", he confessed on a sigh. "It still sounds risky. I may not be a model citizen, but I'm not exactly the kidnapping type, either. Maybe we should take a little more time to—"

"No! We've sat on our asses for too long. *It's. Time.* And if you don't have the balls to help me, then I'll do it myself."

He leaned back on the couch and studied his accomplice. Looks like somebody was suddenly turning a little brave. He should be pissed, really. He didn't necessarily like the concept of the pretty pharmacist accompanying them against her will. But valid points had been made. And as much as he hated to admit it, the proposed plan *was* starting to grow on him.

They'd already spent too much time here—and in this business, staying in one place for too long didn't bode well. It tended to cause suspicion (something they couldn't afford right now).

He wavered for a moment. If this didn't work, they could find themselves in a world of trouble, the police nipping at their heels. But if it did work as planned...? This time next week they could be sipping Coronas in the Caribbean sun on a much-needed—and

well-deserved—vacation, resting up until the next
big job...

"Okay", he conceded. "We'll strike on Friday night.
That gives us four days to prep."

Chapter 24

Kendall parked her Maxima in the driveway after a lengthy four-hour drive from Jacksonville, and an even longer shift behind the pharmacy counter.

Trudging into the kitchen, she removed a bowl from the cupboard and filled it with her favorite orange sherbet ice cream. And because her dinner choice was lacking a vegetable, she reached into the pantry for the bag of salt and vinegar potato chips, and crumbled a handful over the top.

"Perfection in a bowl", she mumbled, as she wiped her hands on a nearby dish towel.

She was pretty certain the strange combination probably wouldn't appeal to her tomorrow. But right now, anyone threatening to come between her and her gourmet creation would likely find themselves spooned to death. Depriving a pregnant woman her biggest craving was justifiable homicide, wasn't it?

Laughing inwardly at her odd train of thought, she grabbed a spoon and headed into the living room. She moaned in delight as the flavors melded in her mouth: cold, sweet, tartness and salty, pungent crunchiness from the potato chips. "Damn, that's good", she whispered softly. She savored the bizarre fusion, resisting the urge to lick the bowl clean with her tongue (because she *did* have *some* limits, for heaven's sake).

After placing the empty bowl on the coffee table, she reached for the *What to Expect When You're Expecting* book she'd purchased on her lunch break two days ago, preparing herself for what lay ahead. She was already ten weeks into her pregnancy— three weeks shy of completing her first trimester. She really needed to hire a replacement soon; the idea of people knowing about her pregnancy— specifically the part about how the father had been married at the time of conception—didn't appeal much. Sure, everyone would find out eventually. She just didn't want to fend off the stares and overhear the whispers firsthand.

Her eyelids drew heavy as she started chapter eight. What a joke this Friday night was turning out to be. Most single girls her age were probably out at a bar, living up the night until they were either cut-off or kicked-out.

But not her. Nope, she'd stuffed her face with ice cream and chips—alone—and was currently reading about constipation. Pathetic, wasn't she?

Kendall skipped over the section about cramps after orgasms. Because (a) orgasms were a luxury no longer afforded to her, and (b) she was so tired she doubted she'd be able to retain anything about the subject now anyway.

Resting the opened book on her chest, she closed her eyes, surrendering to the soothing darkness nipping at her heels. Tomorrow she'd start chapter nine and maybe have a slice of quiche for breakfast

with a heaping dollop of chocolate whipped cream.
Mmmm, now that was a brilliant idea...

The masked criminals waited until eleven-thirty, parking their car one street over from Kendall's house. The trek only took two minutes by foot, and by the time they landed on her front porch, their adrenaline was primed for the mission ahead.

"Remember", the large man reminded, "no talking. She'll recognize your voice."

With a firm nod, the small accomplice shifted the welcome mat, revealing the spare key and accenting the soundness of the proposed plan. After unlocking the door, they eased it open, immediately greeted with the sight of a sleeping Kendall, stretched-out comfortably on the gray sofa.

Quietly, they tiptoed further into the living room, coming to a halt beside her.

The small conspirator's eyes temporarily veered to the open book lying on Kendall's chest.

The fucking whore was pregnant?

Fingers of darkness crept into the short accomplice's vision as rage threatened to boil over.

You have to push it aside—you have to stay in control!

Kendall stirred in her sleep as an eerie sensation swept over her, raising the hair on the back of her neck. And as she opened her heavy lids she was accosted with a familiar image: two masked men— one large, one small—and both aiming handguns at her.

"We meet again", the larger of the men greeted.

Don't panic. They aren't real. Okay, so maybe

the odd combination of ice cream and salt and vinegar Lays weren't such a terrific idea after all. Obviously there were... side effects. Like hallucinations. Because the two images hovering above her couldn't be real. "You're just dreaming", she whispered as she clenched her eyes shut. But her eyes abruptly opened the moment she heard his deep voice again.

"Oh, don't look so scared, sweetheart. We're just going to take a little ride. We'll have you back here in a jiffy."

"No", she uttered softly as her head shook from side-to-side. "No, I'm not going anywhere with"—the small man stepped forward and cocked his gun"—on second thought, a change of scenery sounds nice."

Roughly five minutes later, Kendall parked her car in front of Porter Pharmacy, the dimly lit street lined with various businesses eerily deserted. A ghost town.

There's no knight in shining armor to come to your rescue this time. It's all up to you, now. Don't screw up!

"It's showtime", the large masked-man announced from the passenger seat.

Just then, the small accomplice nudged the muzzle of the handgun against the back of Kendall's skull.

The feel of the cold hard metal—or rather, the fear of the gun discharging a bullet into the back of her head—caused a swell of emotions.

Panic. Anger. Unadulterated fear.

And an overwhelming compulsion to protect the life growing inside her.

Her very first protective motherly instinct...

Emerging from behind the wheel, Kendall cautiously walked around the familiar brick building to the back entrance. She searched for someone—anyone—from the corners of her vision, but it was no use. Neighboring business owners had resigned for the evening hours ago.

She had to do something... But what?

The trio finally reached the back entrance. And with trembling hands, Kendall fit the key into the lock and gave it a twist to the right.

"How much time do we have to disarm the alarm?"

"Fifteen seconds", she replied softly.

"Where's the keypad located?"

"J-just inside. On the left."

"Okay", the larger man muttered. "Go."

Kendall opened the door, separating the sensors, starting the fifteen second countdown.

Rushing forward, she weighed her options. If she let the fifteen seconds expend without disarming the security system, the alarm would sound and the police would be here in minutes. But she'd likely be face down with a bullet lodged in her brain. Scratch that option.

Twelve. Eleven...

She could do as she was told: disarm the alarm. She'd survive this nightmare—the large masked-man assured her she wouldn't be harmed as long as she followed directions. But what if they came back a third time? And what about other potential victims? Could she live guiltlessly knowing these two men were still out there somewhere?—terrorizing other unsuspecting pharmacists?

No. She couldn't do that either.

Nine. Eight...

At that moment, she remembered that the representative from the security company had her select

a special code—a code in case she was asked to disarm
the alarm against her will. Entering this special code
would stop the alarm from blaring, making the
intruders think they were in the clear. But, of course,
they weren't. Because a silent alarm would notify the
police immediately, and within minutes, help would be
on the way.

Five. Four...

The large thief pressed the muzzle of his gun
against her temple. "What're you waiting for? Do it!"

Right hand quivering, Kendall punched in the
special code: 4357 (literally spelling the word "help").
The keypad beeped twice and then an automated
voice confirmed the command by stating, "ALARM DE-
ACTIVATED."

"Alright, you know the drill", the large man
spat as he shoved three sacs toward her. "Fill 'em
up."

Kendall gripped the cloth bags and moved
further into the pharmacy until she came upon the
shelf that housed the pharmacy's supply of controlled substances. Her movements were methodical,
slow—partly because she was terrified, and partly
because her plan wouldn't work if they were already
gone by the time the police arrived.

"Hurry. Up."

"I-I'm trying." She emptied the narcotics into
their respective bags and was just reaching for the
container of Xanax when she heard it.

Sirens.

She paused for a moment, stealing a quick glimpse
of the masked-men over her shoulder as they realized
the police were aware of their presence. She couldn't see
their expressions through the dark masks, but their
eyes were glazed with panic. The sirens were still

distant (weren't the police supposed to respond to events like this silently?) and she knew they'd never arrive in time to save her from a bullet.

"What the hell did you do, Kendall?"

Kendall quickly snapped her head toward the shorter of the two criminals. She knew that voice. And it didn't belong to a man—it was female.

It was Cameron's.

"Cameron?" she whispered incredulously. With her focus on the identity of the small-framed criminal behind the mask, Kendall didn't see the larger man lunge toward her until it was too late. He raised his weapon in the air, striking the butt of the handgun against the upper-right corner of her forehead.

"Look what you made me do!" Jeff shouted. "You weren't supposed to talk, Cammy!

Cameron watched in horror as Kendall's knees buckled, her unconscious body falling to the hard ground, landing with a loud thump. "Omigod, Jeff! She's not dead, is she?" she asked as she stepped toward Kendall's motionless body. Sure, she'd been upset that Ty had chosen Kendall over her, and the discovery of the pregnancy book earlier had exacerbated the anger tenfold. But she hadn't wanted the girl *dead*!

Jeff grabbed her by the elbow and yanked her back. "I didn't hit her *that* hard. C'mon, we have to get outta here!"

Chapter 25

Ty sat alone at the fire station, mindlessly flipping through the channels on the tube. He finally landed on a rerun of *Friends*. He hated that show. Never understood the country's fascination with it. And never understood how that Chandler guy could score with smoking-hot Courtney Cox. That sort of thing just didn't happen in real life. Hell, anything for laughs, right?

He thought about changing the channel again, but ultimately decided against it. There was nothing on worth watching this time of night anyway.

Wouldn't make a bit difference if there was—you haven't been able to concentrate on anything other than Kendall since the bonfire last Saturday.

He'd driven by her house a few nights ago—and had almost talked himself into getting out and knocking on the front door, too—but it'd been late and he figured she'd already been asleep.

He worried about her. Olivia had mentioned how chaotic Kendall's schedule had become. When she wasn't in Jacksonville, she was traveling to and

fro and still had to make time for her responsibilities
at Porter Pharmacy. If she wasn't careful, she was
going to run herself ragged. And that wasn't good for
her or the baby.

Their baby... He couldn't help but smile when
he thought about the miracle they'd created. His
mind immediately flooded with images of Kendall's
normally taut belly swelling with life, carrying his
child. His flesh and blood.

The TV caught his attention again as Jennifer
Aniston and that goofy-looking dude she'd had a
baby with danced and sang Sir Mix-A-Lot's "Baby
Got Back", provoking an innocent laugh from their
infant. He had to admit, it *was* pretty funny. And
just like that, he wondered: what kinds of silly
things would he and Kendall do to hear their son or
daughter laugh?

Ty really needed to talk to her. He wanted to
play an active role in her pregnancy—accompany
Kendall to her doctor appointments, attend child-
birthing classes together. He wanted to be the person
she phoned in the middle of the night when she had
a sudden craving for ice cream—or in her case, onion
rings.

He had no doubt that she'd recite another I-can-
take-care-of-myself speech. But eventually she'd come
to realize that he had no ulterior motives—well,
unless convincing Kendall that he was serious about
the three of them becoming a family, counted.

Ty's radio beeped, signaling the presence of an
emergency. Most likely it wouldn't demand his attention. The department primarily responded to fires
and stranded felines perched on the highest branches
of century-old Live Oaks. The city started outsourcing
ambulatory services last year when a budget crisis

threatened to eliminate several positions from the fire department, as well as B.I.P.D. When the decision had been made to cut hours instead of jobs, the city signed an agreement with a private ambulatory company, assigning Butler Island's fire department the responsibility of only responding to emergencies on an as-needed basis as back-up.

He was just about to lower the volume to his radio when he overheard the dispatcher recite the address: 121 Main Street.

Porter Pharmacy.

"Patient is female, presenting with a head injury; now conscious and responsive..."

Ty leapt from the recliner and sprinted toward the small paramedic vehicle parked in the bay. He barely recalled starting the ignition, or the short two minute drive to the pharmacy. Flashing red and blue lights illuminated the dimly lit street, breathing life into the normally deserted business district.

Shoving the small ambulance into PARK, he grabbed his medic pack and raced toward the brick building, weaving through a mass of police cruisers.

And then he saw her.

Kendall was sitting on the curb next to the police chief, a blanket tossed over her shoulders, her face buried in her hands. Praying his knees wouldn't buckle beneath him, Ty stepped toward her. He had so many questions, and was ready to rapidly fire them at Police Chief Richardson, when a familiar sound diverted his attention: the deep roar of Kendall retching.

The moment Kendall opened her eyes, she realized four things. One: her head throbbed in unison

with her heartbeat, each painful pulse feeling as
though her brain would detonate. Two: this wasn't her
bedroom. Three: her clothes were gone, replaced by a
thin cotton garment with green and blue polka dots.
And most importantly, four: Ty was here, his fingers
intertwined with hers. His head was awkwardly
positioned, resting against the metal rail along the
side of the bed.

His lids were closed, giving her the opportunity to
study his handsome face. His blond hair was di-
sheveled from repeatedly running his fingers through
it. Dark lashes lay motionless along his tanned skin and
a sprinkle of coarse blond hair had sprouted along his
jaw. She remembered how that roughened hair had felt
against her skin: jagged, pleasurable. Kendall allowed
her gaze to settle on his mouth—the same mouth that'd
tasted every inch of her body. She was unprepared for
the surge of heat that'd suddenly burrowed low in her
gut. Fighting the unwanted sensation, she fidgeted,
shifting the mattress and causing those dark lashes of
his to flutter open.

"You alright, Doll?" he inquired in a sexy, sleepy
voice. "How's the head?"

What she wouldn't give to hear that voice first
thing every morning. "It hurts a little"—*okay, a lot*—
"but I'm okay." The details of last night were still a
bit fuzzy, and she hoped Ty would be able to fill in
the gaps. "What happened last night?"

"Do you remember anything?"

"Bits and pieces. I remember driving home from
Jacksonville and falling asleep on the couch. And
then..." Kendall clenched her eyes shut. "I woke up
and they were there."

"That's how they got to you?"

Kendall opened her eyes and nodded, wincing

as the motion rocked her tender brain. "They made me drive them to the pharmacy and had me disarm the—"

"Chief Richardson said you activated the silent alarm. They probably wouldn't have caught up with them if you hadn't done that."

"They found them?" she questioned. He nodded, and suddenly the vacant segments of her memory were filled. "*Cameron...*"

Ty nodded again, squeezing her hand gently as though he was seeking comfort. "Yeah. Apparently the successful businessman she left me for made his fortune stealing prescription narcotics, selling them to the highest bidder..."

"I'm so sorry, Ty."

"Don't be. You have nothing to be sorry—"

"Oh, my God"—she uttered as she clutched her stomach—"the baby—"

"It's okay. The baby's fine", he assured her. And with an ear-to-ear grin, he gently caressed her belly. "I had the chance to hear the heartbeat last night while you were sleeping. It was... it was *amazing.*"

Euphoria radiated off Ty in waves and Kendall took a moment to wallow in it. Took a few extra moments to daydream about what it'd be like for the three of them to become a family... And then realizing how pointless her reverie had been, she accepted the cold hard truth: Ty's role in her life was simply the father of her unborn child—nothing more, nothing less.

"You should probably get some rest, you look tired", he uttered softly.

Between the normal exhaustion of being pregnant, the long roundtrip drive from Jacksonville yesterday, and her mild concussion, she had to admit she *was* tired. But that wasn't the only thing she was tired of. She was tired of pretending. And when her head stopped pounding, she had some serious thinking to do.

Ty stayed by her bedside until the steady rise and fall of her chest assured him she'd fallen asleep. God, when he thought about how he could've lost her last night... Quietly he nudged the door open, looking over his shoulder one last time at the angel with the halo of ink-black hair sleeping comfortably, peacefully.

Stepping into the hallway, Ty tried to reconcile that his ex-wife was responsible for this. What the hell had she been thinking? How could he have slept next to a woman for six years and not see how selfish, conniving, and evil she truly was?

According to Police Chief Richardson, the guns used in the robbery weren't loaded—thank God—and further explained why Kendall had been pistol whipped. At least Cameron and her sidekick had had enough sense to use unloaded weapons. He didn't even want to think about how differently things would've turned out had there been bullets in either of the guns' chambers.

He didn't know how much longer he could carry this façade. Kendall Porter had wriggled her way into his heart, becoming the most important thing in his life. She'd become an addiction of sorts, one he knew he'd never overcome. Because being with her felt good—not just sexually (although that was an added bonus)—but in every other way that really mattered.

He loved her perseverance and ambition. He loved her sarcasm and the way they'd verbally spar over random topics. He loved that she ate bacon cheeseburgers on a regular basis and designated onion rings as the final meal on her hypothetical death row menu. He loved how important her privacy was to her and the way she treated everyone she cared about as though they were important to her, too.

Plainly put: he loved her.

Utterly. Completely. Forever.

Nope, kicking his Kendall Porter addiction was like saying his body could overcome its dependency to oxygen. Both were needed for his existence. He just needed to figure out how he was going to continue getting his fix.

"How is she?" Olivia asked as she and Grant approached.

Ty wiped his palm down his tired face. "Good. She's sleeping now."

"And the baby?"

"He has a strong heartbeat—one-hundred seventy-two beats per minute."

"*He...?*" Grant asked in confusion.

"Call it a gut feeling. Besides", he said as he ruffled the hair on top of Olivia's head, "I've already raised a little girl."

Olivia crossed her arms over her chest. "Hey!—I wasn't *that* bad!"

Ty cocked an eyebrow. "Maybe not at first, but you definitely made up for it later on when you were in high school. I seem to recall an incident with a certain stolen jet ski..."

"*Borrowed* jet ski", she emphasized. "I returned it when I was done."

Grant chuckled under his breath. "I still can't believe that was you." His wife was a legend here on the island, first for taking Mr. Baker's jet ski on a three-hour joyride when she was fifteen, and then again when she was attacked late last fall when she'd captured pictures of the town's arsonist. Unfortunately for Kendall, she too was about to join the notoriety of becoming Butler Island's most recent legendary story. "Unfortunately", because he knew how important privacy was to her.

While his wife chatted with her older brother, Grant took an opportunity to observe his best friend. The man looked exhausted—both from the ordeal of the last twelve hours and the calamity of falling in love with the woman and pretending otherwise. Yeah, he remembered that look: it was only six months ago that he and Livvy had endured a similar set of circumstances. Seemed stubbornness ran heavily in the Everitt bloodline—Lord knows STUBBORN was Olivia's middle name.

Ty and Kendall loved one another. That much became obvious the night of Grant's wedding. Last night was a close call—things could've turned out much differently. Although disasters are rarely welcomed with open arms, sometimes the lessons we learn from them are. And as Olivia had told him many times, *sometimes life's biggest tragedies reward us with life's greatest gift: a second chance.*

A second chance to put one's priorities in order, and to tell the people you love how truly necessary and important they are in your life.

This tragedy would be the defining moment for Ty and Kendall.

Turning to his wife, Grant suggested she stick around in case Kendall awoke. And when she nodded

her agreement, he turned toward his best friend/
brother-in-law. "C'mon, big guy", he said as he slapped
Ty on the back. "You need some caffeine in your system.
And then you need a serious pep talk by yours truly…"

Chapter 26

After five days of mandatory bed rest per Dr. Conrad's orders, Kendall was back into the throes of her chaotic routine. Her day had begun early. Translation: she'd been stuck with the night shift this week at the twenty-four hour Pharm-Aid she'd recently been hired at.

When the clock struck three in the morning, she shuffled into the employee break room and removed the Chinese takeout she'd purchased earlier—technically, last night—from the fridge. She popped the containers in the microwave for a minute, waiting patiently until the appliance nuked her food to the perfect temperature.

Settling into a nearby chair, Kendall ate in silence, listening for the chime that announced the arrival of a customer at the drive-thru window.

Asking for five days off at her new job had been downright embarrassing, but luckily her manager had happily obliged. Seemed everyone here had gone out of their way to accommodate her (well, with the exception of working the night shift, that is). She really appreciated how kind everyone had been and was grateful for the patience management had exercised due to her lingering responsibilities back at Porter Pharmacy. This was supposed to be her dream job. She was supposed to be... happy.

But she wasn't. Not anymore.

Her happiness had ended the morning Cameron appeared at the foot of Ty's bed, dangling her key like she had a right to be there. *She did have a right to be there, because legally Cameron and Ty were still married that morning...*

Finishing her dinner, Kendall eyed the two fortune cookies lying on the table. Craving their light crispy texture—and their wisdom, no doubt—she opened the first wrapper and snapped the cookie in half.

DON'T WAIT FOR YOUR SHIP TO COME IN, SWIM OUT TO IT.

Kendall stared at the small strip of paper in disbelief. "What is it with fortune cookies and their boat metaphors?" she mumbled softly. She thought about what Ty would say. *Sometimes you have to read between the lines. It's not promoting exercise; it's motivating you to chase your dreams...*

Kendall closed her eyes. Hadn't she done that? She'd followed her dreams, landing a job in the state's biggest city. Question was: what if the *ship* she'd tirelessly swam toward turned out to be the wrong one?

Reaching for the second fortune cookie, Kendall tore open the package and snapped the treat in half. Taking in a liter of air, she willed herself to look at the message typed on the small strip of paper. But she was unprepared for the omen staring back at her.

YOU CREATE YOUR OWN STAGE. YOUR AUDIENCE IS WAITING...

It was then she realized what she had to do.

She had to jump back into the water and swim to shore. And then she had a lengthy monologue to prepare for.

Ty studied the illustration on the instruction manual. According to the directions, he was supposed to fit part EE into the groove of part W, and then fasten the two parts together with a screw labeled Q. Although he was pretty certain he'd used Q three steps back.

"Ah, shit..."

Yep, this was going to take a while. Good thing his kid wouldn't need a crib until November. Because it just might take him that long to assemble it.

Opting for a break, Ty trudged into the kitchen and snagged a cold beer from the fridge. He twisted the top and then took a long satisfying gulp. *Great. Barely noon and you're already drowning your sorrows.*

It'd been almost a week since he'd discovered Kendall on the curb in front of Porter Pharmacy, with a mild concussion and a goose egg the size of Texas. He allowed himself to relive the moment again: the terror of racing toward her, unaware of the extent of her injuries, and the relief that'd washed over him the instant he was told the trauma she'd sustained hadn't been life-threatening.

Sometimes life's biggest tragedies reward us

with life's greatest gift: a second chance. Grant had reiterated this during his "pep talk." And it was true. His little sister captured catastrophes through the lens of her camera for a living and had recited this sentence to him for years. *Never take for granted what you treasure most. And when life gifts you with a second chance: take it.*

Kendall had been released twenty-four hours after her arrival at Mainland Hospital and had returned home—her childhood home. He'd visited everyday during her ordered bed rest, wanting to share how he'd been living a lie. Wanting to confess that he'd fallen in love with her. But the opportunity had never presented itself. Confessing his love in front of Mr. and Mrs. Porter hadn't sat well with him.

Well, that's not entirely true. It wasn't so much the confessing part that had him tied in knots; it was the part that came after. The part where Kendall— and her parents—reacted to the broadcast...

It was then that Ty was reminded of something else Grant had said. *Swallow your pride—beg if you have to. Because a few moments of awkwardness are worth the lifetime of happiness you'll gain.*

And Ty knew he wouldn't be happy until Kendall was more than the woman he'd once had a one-day-at-a-time arrangement with—more than the mother of his child.

Tossing his head back, he chugged the remains of his Bud Light, praying a slight buzz would ignite the courage needed for what he would do in a few hours when she returned from Jacksonville.

No more excuses.

When he laid his head on his pillow tonight, the way he felt about Kendall Porter would be out in the open. And then the ball would be in *her* court.

A faint knock sounded at the door. Ty figured it had to be one of the guys from the department—Olivia was out of town on an assignment and everybody else he hung out with was still at work. Setting his empty beer bottle on the counter, Ty trekked toward the door and opened it.

A dark-haired woman stood with her back turned. He didn't see her face, but he didn't need to—he'd recognize that body anywhere. *"Kendall...?"*

She kept her back turned, staring at the large cardboard box sitting on the curb. The one with a picture of a baby crib printed on the front. "You bought a crib", she whispered.

"Yeah."

Slowly, she turned to face him. He wore his faded Levi's low on his hips and a plain white T-shirt that stretched across his broad chest, showcasing every ridge and valley of his toned physique. Her eyes continued their journey north, noting that he hadn't shaved, and then settled on a pair of Peridot peepers staring back at her. "Is this a bad time?—I can come back later if—"

"No", he responded quickly as he reached for her hand and tugged her inside. He shut the door behind them with his free hand, unwilling to extricate his fingers from her grasp just yet. "Everything okay?—feeling alright?"

Kendall nodded. "I'm fine... You sure this isn't a bad time?"

Ty swept a lock of black hair from her left eye and smiled. "I'm glad you came." He studied the face of the woman that'd haunted his dreams for the past month. This was it. This was the moment he'd been waiting for. He opened his mouth, but instead of telling Kendall that he loved her, he asked if she was thirsty. *What the hell?*

Licking her suddenly dry lips, she answered, "Bottled water, please; if you have one." Because she couldn't proceed with the monologue she'd tenaciously rehearsed during the long, four-hour drive from Jacksonville if her tongue was glued to the roof of her mouth.

"I do. C'mon on."

Kendall followed him into the kitchen, noting the empty beer bottle on the counter. "Rough morning?" she asked as she gestured toward the Bud Light.

Ty grabbed a bottle of water and another beer from the fridge, then handed her the plastic container. He twisted the cap and took a long pull of cold frothy liquid and then motioned for her to follow him outside on the patio. "I guess you could say that. I'm good at a lot of things, but assembling furniture's definitely not one of them."

"That bad, huh?"

"I'm afraid so."

Kendall took a sip of water, allowing her eyes to scan over the backyard. The lofty Live Oak shaded much of the yard, its branches swaying gracefully in the light breeze. The grass appeared to have been recently mowed and the hibiscus plants along the wood privacy fence were in full bloom, vivid splashes of red welcoming the summer ahead. And when her focus settled on the rectangular pool, she suddenly realized something was different. "You had a pool fence installed?"

Ty glanced over his shoulder and then met her gaze. "Can't have our little boy fallin' in. Besides, the fence company was running a special."

She felt a small flutter reside deep in her chest as her heart expanded with love and adoration. But she couldn't dwell on that right now. At least not until she'd successfully recited the monologue she'd rehearsed. *Stay on track.*

"Little boy? You're awfully confident."

"So I've been told..." Kendall rolled her eyes playfully and then took another sip of water. "How's the new job?" he inquired.

"It's, um... well, that's sort of why I'm here. The position at Porter Pharmacy's been filled. And I wanted to tell you in person that—"

"Wait", he interrupted. "There's something you need to know. Something I've been meaning to say to you since—"

Kendall held her hand in front of her, silencing him in mid-sentence. "Please let me finish—before I lose the nerve." She waited a few moments as he studied her. And when he finally nodded, she took a deep breath, placing her water bottle beside her on the patio table. "Okay... I decided to remain full-time at Porter Pharmacy."

"You can't do that—you'll tire yourself out working here and in Jacksonville indefinitely. It's not healthy for you or—"

Kendall held her palm out again. "I'm not finished." Ty wiped his hand down his face and gestured for her to continue. "I spoke with my manager this morning. And I convinced him that it was in Pharm-Aid's best interest to hire someone else."

"You quit?"

Nodding, she answered, "Yes."

Ty's brows trenched in confusion. "But you always wanted to—"

"I've had a lot of time to think the last few days. And I realized how much I missed standing behind the counter at Porter Pharmacy. Seeing familiar faces... Pharm-Aid just wasn't like that. It was... impersonal, I guess."

"Well, I'm glad you're stickin' around, because—"

Kendall raised her palm in front of her again. "Wait, there's more... There's another reason why I decided to stay in Butler Island. It's..." Kendall drew in a shaky breath and then pursed her lips together, slowly releasing it. "Well... it's *you*. I went into this knowing the terms. I knew what we were and what we weren't. I knew at some point I'd find myself at a crossroads. For me, that moment came the night I surprised you at the fire station.

"I went there with the intention of proving to myself that what I felt for you was purely physical. But I left that night with more than I bargained for. That was the night we created life... And it was also when I accepted what I'd been denying for weeks. I'm... I'm in love with you", she finally blurted.

Ty stood motionless, his jaw slack; his eyes wide with disbelief. *Had he heard her right? She loved him?*

Kendall gnawed nervously on her bottom lip, perusing his bewildered expression for clues as to what he was thinking. "Say something", she whispered. When he didn't, she started rambling. "Oh, that's just perfect. You've interrupted me three times and when I'm finally ready to let you speak, you've got nothing to say!" Kendall covered her face with her hands. "This isn't how I pictured it in my head. You were supposed to—"

Ty sat his beer on the patio table and peeled her hands away from her face. He wrestled them behind her back and then covered her mouth with his.

Kendall's lips parted on a sigh, and he took the opportunity to show her the words that'd failed him moments earlier. Every tender sweep of his tongue was meant to reassure her. And within moments, her body softened against him, surrendering.

Kendall untangled her hands from Ty's grasp and palmed his face, releasing a month's worth of pent-up passion.

Raptured in the moment, Ty knew he would never tire of kissing this woman. But before this went any further, she needed to hear his response to her admission.

He separated their lips, resting his forehead against hers. "I love you, too. I'm not sure when it happened exactly, but I do know the last month without you nearly killed me. I'm addicted to you, Kendall Porter—addicted to the way you make me feel when I'm with you—"

"Ty, I—"

Mimicking her earlier gesture, Ty placed a finger over her mouth to silence her. "Shhh. I'm not done yet."

She smiled. "Alright, go on..."

"I want us to be a family: me, you... and junior", he uttered with a smirk as he rubbed her belly. "I want to eat bacon cheeseburgers and onion rings with you. I want to kiss you at the stroke of midnight on every New Year's Eve. And I want your beautiful face to be the first thing I see every morning when I open my eyes..."

Kendall's vision blurred (damn pregnancy hormones). Unable to suppress the emotions swelling inside her, tears rained down her face.

Swiping their path with his thumb, Ty gazed

into the eyes of the woman he loved. "Happy tears?" he questioned hopefully. She nodded. "So, how 'bout it? Are you gonna provide me with my drug of choice?"

"And what is your drug of choice?"

Ty smiled. "You. Every day. Forever..."

Kendall raked her teeth against her bottom lip. "Only under two conditions", she said as she gestured with her fingers.

"Alright, what are the new terms?"

"One: I have to be your only dealer—"

"—Done', he interrupted again.

"And two: this"—she gestured between them— "has to be more than physical. I need all of you, Ty. I need... *all of you.*"

"You already have that; you just didn't know it until now", he whispered as he tucked a strand of hair behind her ear.

"I love you, Ty Everitt."

Those simple words held more meaning than anything she'd ever said. They'd been given a second chance. A fresh start. And this time, he wouldn't take one moment for granted. "I love you, too. *Both of you.*"

No doubt about it: Ty was addicted to Kendall Porter. He craved her—his body's dependency was on a cellular level. The high he experienced was too powerful—too pleasurable—to quit. The disease had conquered him...

And he never wanted to be cured.

Epilogue

The baby monitor carried the unmistakable sound of an infant crying, causing both Kendall and Ty to stir. Rolling to his side, he caressed her bare shoulder with his knuckles and then planted a kiss to her temple. "I've got it this time", he whispered softly. "Go back to sleep, Doll."

Ty shuffled into the kitchen in the dark, wincing when the light from the refrigerator spilled into the room, stinging his sensitive orbs. With one eye closed, he snatched the ready-made bottle from the top shelf and proceeded to warm the milk, making sure to test the temperature of the formula on the inside of his wrist.

Satisfied with the result, Ty retraced his steps back into the hallway, nudged the nursery door open, and scooped his little girl into his arms.

"Hey there, Princess; it's daddy."

His precious little angel latched onto the bottle's nipple as he settled into the nearby rocking chair. He listened to the melody of slurping, swallowing; the innocent sounds filling the dimly lit lady bug nursery.

He rocked her—for how long, he couldn't say—
but the bottle was empty and her lids seemed to grow
heavy as they swayed. Back. Forth. Back. Forth.

When he thought about the events that'd led
him to this very moment, he couldn't help but smile.
His baby girl was perfect—beautiful. Just like her
momma.

They'd named her Tenley: *Tenley Kay Everitt.*

She'd kept everyone waiting two very long
weeks past Kendall's due date before making her
grand entrance, but seeing the woman he loved
holding their miracle had been well worth it.

It was at that moment he finally understood
what it meant to fall in love at first sight. The
moment he laid eyes on Tenley, he was a goner. She
had a headful of thick black hair, Kendall's pouty
lips, and the tiniest ten fingers and ten toes he'd
ever seen. Her eyes had been blue at birth, but were
slowly transforming into a familiar shade of amber.

"Is she sleeping?" Kendall asked as she quietly
tiptoed into the nursery.

Ty glanced at the precious angel swaddled in his
arms. "Think so", he whispered. Rising from the rocking
chair, he carefully placed Tenley back into her crib—*the
crib he and Kendall had assembled together*—making
sure the gentle motion hadn't disrupted her peaceful
dreams.

Kendall reached for his hand and tugged, leading
him out of the nursery. But instead of turning right
toward the master suite, they made a left.

"What are we doing?" he finally asked as they
crept into the dark kitchen.

"You'll see."

Twisting the deadbolt with her free hand, she
opened the French door that led to the patio, stepping

onto the cool concrete with her bare feet. She hauled him past the rectangular pool until they reached the middle of the backyard.

Ty carefully analyzed his wife as she concentrated on her watch. She studied the damn thing as though she expected the leather band to suddenly grow teeth and sink its fangs into her soft flesh. "Alright, you're really starting to freak me out a little, Doll. You do realize we're barefoot in the backyard in the middle of the night, right?"

Nothing. No response. She just kept staring at that damn watch.

"We should be back in bed sleeping. *Or...*"

Still nothing.

"You must be sleepwalking", he finally decided. "I've read about this before. Okay, I remember reading that you're never supposed to wake a sleepwalker. Instead, you—"

"I'm not sleepwalking", she uttered as she glanced away from her watch, acknowledging his presence for the first time since they'd ventured outside. "It's New Year's Eve, remember? And we're roughly fifteen seconds from midnight."

Ten, nine, eight...

Ty tugged on her waist, pulling her body against his. "Trying to fulfill another one of those *fantasies* again, Doll?"

Kendall's hands traveled up his bare chest. "Fantasies aren't all they're cracked up to be."

"Really?" he asked, unconvinced.

"No. Reality is *much* better."

Ty flashed his signature, sexy grin as his mouth drew closer to hers.

Three, two, one...

"Happy New Year, Mrs. Everitt."

Nikki Rittenberry's

Next Butler Island Series Book

Rescue Me

Please visit www.nikkirittenberry.com for a complete booklist, news about upcoming novels, and the author's bio.